The Wrestling Princess

AND OTHER STORIES

"I *don't* want a husband," said the princess and she stamped her foot hard. The toast rack wobbled. "*You* want me to have a husband. I just want to go on wrestling and looking after my trucks and driving in parades."

"Well, you can't," said the king. "And that's that. I shall lock up the forklift trucks and tell the guards there is to be no more wrestling. And we shall have a contest to find you a husband."

The princess was furious.

"Just you wait," she yelled rudely, "I'll ruin your stupid old contest. How dare you lock up my forklift trucks. You're a rotten mean old pig!"

"Ermyntrude," said the king, "you will do as you are told

Also available in Hippo Funny:

Shoot, Dad!
Michael Coleman

The Dreaded Lurgie
Jamie Rix

**The Amazing Adventures
of Raincoat Man**
Brandon Robshaw

Agnes the Sheep
William Taylor

HIPPO FUNNY

The Wrestling Princess

AND OTHER STORIES

Judy Corbalis

Illustrations by Helen Craig

Hippo

For Toby, Jemima, Jerome, Katya and Helen

Scholastic Children's Books
Commonwealth House, 1-19 New Oxford Street,
London WC1A 1NU, UK
a division of Scholastic Ltd
London ~ New York ~ Toronto ~ Sydney ~ Auckland

First published by André Deutsch Ltd, 1986
This edition published by Scholastic Ltd, 1997

Text copyright © Judy Corbalis, 1986
Illustrations copyright © Helen Craig, 1986

ISBN 0 590 19321 X

Typeset by TW Typesetting, Midsomer Norton, Somerset
Printed by Cox & Wyman Ltd, Reading, Berks.

10 9 8 7 6 5 4 3 2 1

CONTENTS

THE WRESTLING PRINCESS

Once upon a time there was a princess who was two metres tall, who liked her own way and who loved to wrestle. Every day, she would challenge the guards at her father's palace to wrestling matches and every day, she won. Then she would pick up the loser and fling him on the ground. But gently, because she had a very kind nature.

The princess had one other unusual hobby. She liked to drive forklift trucks. Because she was a princess, and her father was very rich, she had three forklift trucks of her own — a blue one, a yellow one, and a green and purple striped one with a crown on each side.

1

Whenever there was a royal parade, the king would ride in front in his golden carriage, behind him would ride a company of soldiers and behind them came the princess driving her striped royal forklift truck. The king got very cross about it but the princess simply said, "If I can't drive my forklift truck, I won't go," and because she was such a good wrestler, the king was too scared to disagree with her.

One day, when the princess had wrestled with sixteen soldiers at once and had beaten them all, the king sent a page to tell her to come to see him in the royal tea-room.

The princess was annoyed.

"Is it urgent?" she asked the page. "I'm greasing the axle of my blue forklift truck."

"You ought to come, Your Highness," said the page. "His Majesty's in a terrible temper. He's burnt four pieces of toast already and dripped butter all over his second-best ermine robe."

"Drat," said the princess, "I'd better come right away."

So she got up, picked up her oil-can and went into the royal bathroom to wash her hands for tea. She left oil marks all over the gold taps and the page sent a message to the palace housekeeper to clean them quickly before the king saw them.

The princess ran down to the tea-room and banged on the door. A herald opened it. "The Princess Ermyntrude!" he announced.

"About time, too," said the king. "Where have you been?"

"Greasing the axle of my blue forklift truck," said the princess.

The king put his head in his hands.

"This can't go on," he groaned. "When *will* you stop messing about with these dirty machines, Ermyntrude? You're nearly sixteen, you need a husband. I must have a successor."

"I'll succeed you, father," said the princess. "I'd love to be king."

"*You* can't be king," said the king. "It's not allowed."

"Why not?"

"I don't know," said the king. "I don't make the laws. Ask the judges – it's their affair. Anyway, you can't and that's that. You have to have a husband."

He picked up his tapestry and moodily started sewing.

"And," he said, "you won't get a husband if you don't change your ways."

The princess was surprised.

"Why ever not?"

"To get a husband you must be enchantingly beautiful, dainty and weak," said the king.

Ermyntrude grinned. "Well, I'm not," she said. "I'm nothing to look at, I'm two metres tall and I'm certainly not weak. This morning I wrestled with sixteen guards at once and I defeated them all."

"Ermyntrude!" said the king sternly, as he rethreaded his needle with No. 9 blue tapestry cotton. "We are not having any more wrestling and no more forklift trucks either. If you want a husband, you will have to become delicate and frail."

"I *don't* want a husband," said the princess and she stamped her foot hard. The toast rack wobbled. "*You* want me to have a husband. I just want to go on wrestling and looking after my trucks and driving in parades."

"Well, you can't," said the king. "And that's

4

that. I shall lock up the forklift trucks and tell the guards there is to be no more wrestling. And we shall have a contest to find you a husband."

The princess was furious.

"Just you wait," she yelled rudely, "I'll ruin your stupid old contest. How dare you lock up my forklift trucks. You're a rotten mean old pig!"

"Ermyntrude," said the king, putting down his tapestry, "you will do as you are told." And he got up and left the royal tea-room.

The princess was very very angry. She bent the toasting fork in half and stamped all over the bread.

"Stupid, stupid, stupid," she shouted. And she went away to think out a plan.

The first contest to find a prince to marry the Princess Ermyntrude took place next day. The king had beamed a message by satellite to all the neighbouring countries and helicopters with eligible princes in them were arriving in droves at the palace heliport.

The princess watched them from the window of her room where she was sulking.

"Stupid, stupid," she muttered. "Look, not one of them can even pilot his own helicopter."

And she went on sulking.

After lunch, the king sent a messenger to tell the princess to dress in her best robes and come to the great hall of the palace.

She put on her golden dress and her fur cape and her small golden crown and her large golden shoes (for she had big feet) and down she went.

At the door of the throne room she stopped to give the herald time to announce her name, then she strode in.

Seated inside were seventy-two princes, each seeking her hand in marriage.

The princess looked at them all. They all looked back.

"Sit here, my dear," said the king loudly, and under his breath, he added, "and behave yourself!"

The princess said nothing.

"Good afternoon and welcome to you all," began the king. "We are here today to find a suitable husband for my daughter, the lovely Princess Ermyntrude. There will be three contests and the winner of them all will have the princess as his bride.

"The first contest will be that of height. As you know the princess is a very tall girl. She cannot have a husband shorter than herself so you will all line up while the Lord Chamberlain measures you."

The seventy-two princes lined up in six rows and the Lord Chamberlain took out the royal tape measure and began to measure them.

"Why can't I have a shorter husband?" whispered the princess.

"Be quiet," said the king. "You just can't."

"Forty-eight princes left in the contest, Your Majesty," said the Lord Chamberlain.

"Thank you," said the king. "I'm sorry you gentlemen had a wasted journey but you are welcome at the banquet this evening." And he bowed very low.

"And now for the second contest. It will be that of disposition. The Princess Ermyntrude has a beautiful nature, none better, but she does have a slightly hasty temper. She cannot have a husband who is unable to match her temper, so we shall have a face-pulling, insult-throwing contest. The Lord Chamberlain will call your names one by one, you will come forward and confront the princess, pull the worst face you can manage, put on a temper display and insult her."

"Your Majesty, is this wise? Twenty-four of the princes have given up at the thought of it," hisscd the Lord Chamberlain.

"Weaklings," murmured the princess.

The first prince stepped forward. The Princess Ermyntrude pulled a repulsive face and he burst into tears.

"Eliminated," called the Lord Chamberlain, running forward with a box of tissues. "Next!"

The next prince, and the next after him, and the prince following *them*, were all eliminated and it was not until the fifth competitor's turn that anyone succeeded at all. He crossed his eyes, stuck out his tongue and shouted, "Silly cry-baby," at the princess, making her so angry that she forgot to shout back.

The fifth prince inspired the next four after him. But the princes after that were no match for Princess Ermyntrude until the eighteenth and nineteenth princes called her "Crow face" and "Squishy bum" and made her giggle.

By the end of the contest, there were seven princes left, all taller and more insulting than the princess.

"And now," said the king, "for the third and final contest. Strength! As you may know, the Princess Ermyntrude is very strong. She cannot have a weaker husband so you will all line up and wrestle with her."

"Why can't I have a weaker husband?" whispered the princess.

"Be quiet," said the king. "You just can't."

So the Lord Chamberlain lined up the seven princes and as they were being given their instructions, the princess, who was flexing her arm muscles, peered over at the watching crowd of commoners and noticed a short man covered in helicopter engine oil standing at the back. Because she was so tall, she could see him clearly and, as she stared, he looked back at her and winked. The princess looked again. The short man winked again.

"*Helicopter* engine oil!" thought the princess. "That's the sort of man I like."

Just then the short man gave her a secret

wave and mouthed, "Choose the seventh prince. Don't beat *him*."

The princess was intrigued. She watched as the little man pointed discreetly to the tall, nervous-looking prince at the end of the line-up. "That one."

Princess Ermyntrude didn't much like the look of the seventh prince but she did want to please the helicopter mechanic, so she nodded, rolled up her golden sleeves and stepped forward to take on the first prince.

CRASH! He hit the mat with staggering force.

CRASH, CRASH, CRASH, CRASH, CRASH.

The next five princes followed. The poor seventh prince was looking paler and paler and his knees were beginning to buckle under him. The princess glanced at the mechanic, then moved towards the seventh prince. He seized her feebly by the arm.

"I could knock him down with one blow," thought the princess, but she didn't. Instead, she let herself go limp and floppy and two seconds later, for the first time in her life, she

lay flat on her back on the floor.

The crowd let out a stupendous cheer. The king and the Lord Chamberlain rushed forward and seized the hands of the young prince.

The poor prince went white.

"This is terrible, terrible," he muttered.

"Nonsense," cried the king. "I award you the hand of the princess and half my kingdom."

"But Sire…" stammered the prince. "I can't."

"Can't!" shouted the king. "What do you mean can't. You can and you will or I'll have you beheaded!"

There was a scuffle in the crowd and the helicopter mechanic darted forward and bent low at the king's feet.

"Majesty," he said, "I am the prince's helicopter pilot, mechanic and aide. Prince Florizel is overcome with shock and gratitude." He turned to the prince. "Is that not so, Sire?"

"Um, yes, yes, that's right," agreed the prince.

The mechanic smiled.

"Before the ceremony can take place, Prince Florizel must have the blessing of *his* father, the King of Buzzaramia, whose kingdom adjoins your own."

"Quite, quite," said the king. "I favour these old customs myself. The princess will fly there tomorrow to meet her new royal father-in-law."

"And I'll be piloting myself," said the princess.

"We shan't go into *that* now," said the king. "Here, you may kiss the princess."

With a small sigh, the prince fainted dead away.

"Shock," said the pilot hastily. "Clearly shock, Your Majesty. It's not every day he wins the hand of someone so beautiful, charming and talented."

And he looked deep into the princess's eyes.

The prince was carried out to his helicopter and flown off.

The rest of the contestants and the princess had a large and elegant banquet with a six-metre chocolate cake in the shape of a heart and litres of ice-cream.

"Who made that heart?" asked Ermyntrude.

"I ordered it from Cook," said the king.

"Well, *I* think it's soppy. A heart!" said the

princess in disgust.

Next morning she was up early and, dressed in her frog-green flying suit and bright red aviator goggles, she slipped out to her helicopter before the king was up. She was just warming up the engine when the Lord Chamberlain came rushing out into the garden.

"Stop, stop," he cried, waving his arms wildly. "His Majesty, your father, is coming too."

The Princess Ermyntrude turned off the master switch and leaned out of the window.

"Well, he'd better hurry and I'm piloting," she said. "I'll wait three minutes and I'm going if he hasn't come by then."

The Lord Chamberlain rushed into the palace and returned with the king, who was dragging his ermine robe over his nightshirt.

"You're a dreadful girl, Ermyntrude," he said. "Here I am with a hangover from the chocolate cake and you insist on being selfish."

"I'm *not* selfish," said Ermyntrude. "I'm the best pilot in the palace and it's your own fault you've got a hangover if you will let Cook put rum in the chocolate cake. Anyway, all this was your idea. I'm not marrying that silly prince and I'm flying over to tell him so."

The king was scandalized. "How can you do such a thing?" he cried. "I'll be ruined. He won the contest. And besides, you've got to marry someone."

"I haven't and I won't," said the princess and she set the rotor blades in action.

Within an hour, they were flying into the next kingdom and soon they could see the palace shining golden on the highest hilltop.

"Over there," sighed the king. "Please change your mind, Ermyntrude."

"Never," said the princess. "Never, never, never, never, never."

Below them they could see the landing pad with ostrich feathers and fairy-lights along the strip.

Princess Ermyntrude settled the helicopter gently on the ground, waited for the blades to stop turning and got out.

The prince's mechanic was standing on the tarmac.

"A perfect landing," he said admiringly.

The Princess Ermyntrude smiled. Just then,

an older man in ermine-trimmed pyjamas came running across the grass.

"Florizel, what *is* all this?" he called.

The mechanic picked up an oil-can from beside his feet.

"Put that down, you ninny," said the man in ermine pyjamas. "Don't you realize this is a royal princess?"

"You're being ridiculous, Father," said the mechanic. "Of course I realize she's a princess. I'm going to marry her."

"*You* are?" said Princess Ermyntrude's father. "My daughter's not marrying you. She's marrying your prince."

"I am marrying him," said the Princess Ermyntrude.

"She certainly is," said the mechanic. "And, by the way, I *am* Prince Florizel."

"What?" said the princess.

"It was my father's idea that I should enter the competition," said Prince Florizel. "I didn't want to go at all. So I persuaded my mechanic to change places with me. I thought my father would never find out. Then, when I saw the Princess Ermyntrude, I fell instantly in love with her. She had axle grease on her neck and she was so big and strong. And I realized it was lucky I'd changed places or you'd have eliminated me on height."

"That's right," said the king. "You're too short."

"He's not," said the princess.

"No, I'm not, I'm exactly the right size and so is she," said Prince Florizel. "And then, when I saw her pulling faces and shouting insults and throwing princes to the ground, I knew she was the only person I could ever fall in love with."

"Really?" said the princess.

"Truly," said Prince Florizel. "Now, come and see my mechanical digger."

And holding the oil-can in one hand and the princess's hand in the other, he led the way to the machine shed.

The king looked at Prince Florizel's father.

"There's nothing I can do with Ermyntrude once she's made up her mind," he said wearily.

"I have the same trouble with Florizel," said the other king. "I say, would you like an Alka Seltzer and some breakfast?"

"Would I?" said the princess's father. "I

certainly would."

And, arm-in-arm, they went off together to the palace.

And so Princess Ermyntrude and Prince Florizel were married in tremendous splendour.

The Princess Ermyntrude had a special diamond-and-gold-thread mechanic's suit made for the wedding and she drove herself to the church in a beautiful bright red forklift truck with garlands of flowers on the forks, and E in flashing lights on one side and F picked out in stars on the other.

Prince Florizel, who had parachuted in for the wedding, wore an emerald-and-silver thread shirt with silver lamé trousers and had flowers in his beard. On the steps of the church he reached up on tiptoe to kiss the princess as the television cameras whirred and the people cheered, then they ran down the steps and jumped into the royal forklift and steered away through the excited crowds.

"I'm terribly happy," said the prince.

"So am I," said the princess. "I say, did you bring the burgers and the ketchup?"

"All there in the back," said the prince.

"And I've brought the wedding cake," said the princess. "Look."

"Wow," cried Prince Florizel. "It's magnificent."

For the wedding cake was shaped like a giant oil-can.

"Perfect, don't you think?" said the princess.

"Absolutely," said the prince.

And they both lived happily ever after.

THE MAGIC PARROT

Aunt Hilda was at home when Sam came in after school. He'd been hoping she'd be out but she was standing in the hallway with her beady black eyes snapping.

"Just look at the mud on your trousers," she said crossly. "Wipe your feet well."

Sam kept his hands behind his back.

"What have you got behind your back, Sam?" asked Aunt Hilda.

"Nothing," said Sam. "Just a box, that's all."

"Nonsense!" Aunt Hilda was scornful. "Nobody goes round collecting empty boxes. What's in it?"

"Nothing," said Sam again.

"Well, put it on the hall table, then," she said, "and go in and get your tea quietly and quickly. I have a dreadful headache."

Aunt Hilda was always suffering from bad headaches. Sam had to be quiet in the house and tiptoe around and remember not to slam doors, and he could never ever have other children in to play because their noise might disturb Aunt Hilda and make her headaches worse.

He put his box down carefully on the table and, crossing his fingers, he began to open the kitchen door.

Aunt Hilda looked at the box. Sam looked at Aunt Hilda. Very slowly the lid rose and out peeped a tiny brown face with little pointed ears and long long whiskers.

Aunt Hilda screamed and screamed. She rushed upstairs crying and shouting.

"Take it away! Get rid of it *at once*, you horrid, wicked boy."

Poor Sam seized the little hamster and, tucking it into his coat pocket, went into the kitchen and sadly ate his tea. The hamster climbed out of his pocket and sat on the table.

Sam gave it some breadcrumbs and stroked its head. The hamster sat up and looked at him. Its fur was all soft and fluffy.

"She'll never let me keep it now," thought Sam. Then he wondered whether, if he promised to keep the hamster in his room and never let it downstairs, Aunt Hilda and Uncle George might, just this once, let him have a pet.

He sat stroking the hamster for a long time until finally he heard Uncle George's key in the front door. He could hear voices on the stairs, Aunt Hilda's loud and angry, Uncle George's lower and soothing. Uncle George's footsteps came towards the kitchen. Sam put the hamster back in his pocket and put his hand over it to keep it safe.

The door opened.

Uncle George stood there looking furious.

"Sam," he thundered, "I am extremely angry with you. You've upset your aunt and told her a lie. And you've brought a rodent into this house."

"It *isn't* a rodent," said Sam. "It's a baby hamster. This boy at school gave it to me. I'll look after it myself and it doesn't eat much and I'll pay for it out of my pocket money. *Please, please*, Uncle George."

"Certainly not. What an idea!" snorted Uncle George. "Hamsters *are* rodents: they're dirty and unpleasant and you're not keeping one here. Take it straight back to that boy! And as soon as you're home, go upstairs and apologize to your aunt."

And he went out.

Sam sat at the table looking at his hamster with tears in his eyes. He wanted a pet so much. He wasn't allowed a dog or a cat, Uncle George had said a rabbit or a guinea pig would smell, and this hamster had seemed so perfect.

The hamster began to wash its face with its paws.

"I wish I could keep you," said Sam. And he tucked it back in his pocket and slowly set off with it.

When he got home again, he went straight out to the far end of the back garden and climbed up the old apple tree. As he sat there feeling sad and lonely, he heard footsteps. Looking up at him was Blackbeard Smith, his aunt and uncle's gardener.

Blackbeard Smith lived in the big shed at the bottom of the lawn. He kept the garden tidy and cleaned the car and did odd jobs round the house. Aunt Hilda didn't like him at all.

"It's ridiculous having a gardener like that. Of course he can't work properly," she said.

For the really interesting thing about Blackbeard Smith, apart from his wooden leg and the hook he had instead of a hand, was that he was a real live retired pirate. Sam had seen it on one of his letters once.

"B.B. Smith
Pirate (Retd.)"

Aunt Hilda wanted to get rid of Blackbeard, but he came with the house.

"You can't do it, I'm afraid, my dear," Uncle George always said.

Sam was strictly forbidden to go near Blackbeard's shed or to "bother" him at all but, in fact, he quite often talked to Blackbeard while the pirate was working in the garden, and he had a secret ambition to see inside the shed. Blackbeard was tall with a bushy beard and one glittering eye. Sam felt it would have been terrifying to have met him in his pirate clothes.

"Did you have a sword between your teeth?" he asked Blackbeard once.

"Did I? Did I ever, young lad," roared Blackbeard. "A sword in me teeth and another in me hand and a revolver in me belt."

Sam had shuddered with fright at the thought.

Another mysterious thing about Blackbeard Smith was where he went for his holidays. Every year, he would pack up a case and leave for a holiday. He always came back, but he would never say where he'd been. Aunt Hilda got very cross.

"How ridiculous," she said. "Of course we should know where he's going. What if there's an emergency?"

But there never was and Blackbeard Smith would never tell.

"I'm staying with an old friend," was all he would say.

Sam looked at the pirate through the branches.

Blackbeard Smith winked up at him.

"It's a beautiful evening," he said.

Sam glowered down. "No, it's not."

Blackbeard Smith ran his hook menacingly across the tree trunk.

"Sulking, are we?" he said. "Moody, are we? What's on our mind, then? Come down and tell the scourge of the South Sea Clippers what the matter is."

Sam crawled unhappily down the tree trunk.

"I'm in the wrong family," he muttered. "I hate them."

"One way or another," said Blackbeard Smith, "we're all in the wrong family. So what's the problem with them now?"

"They won't let me keep my hamster," blurted out Sam, and he began to cry. "I haven't got *any* pets. Not a white mouse, not a kitten, not nothing."

"Not *anything*," corrected Blackbeard. "You may not have a pet, you may be disappointed in life, but for goodness' sake speak proper, boy."

Sam sniffed.

"You'd better come in and sit down and we'll see what we can come up with," said Blackbeard, and he led Sam into his big shed.

This was the moment Sam had been dreaming of for months.

They stepped inside and Sam saw that the shed was divided into three rooms. Blackbeard pushed open a door and Sam was inside the first retired pirate's sitting room he'd ever seen in his life.

"I don't believe it," he breathed.

"Look around, look around," said Blackbeard expansively. "I'll just go off and slip into something more comfortable."

And while Sam tried the telescope and inspected the room generally, the old pirate stumped off to his back room.

Five minutes later he was back.

Sam stared open-mouthed at his pirate clothes.

"And this," announced Blackbeard Smith, pulling a photograph from behind the armadillo shell, "is my former parrot, Cocky Smart, Retired."

"Retired where?" Sam was curious.

"Where?" cried Blackbeard Smith. "This boy asks me where! Now where would you think a parrot would retire to? Eastbourne?

Too northerly! Blackpool? Too political! Chipping Sodbury? Too rural! The Zoo? Of course not! Use your intelligence, boy. Where would a parrot retire to?"

"I don't know," said Sam.

"The West Indies, of course. Where else? Set himself up nicely in a banana tree near Kingston. Got himself a pretty wife and a fine clutch of eggs, which hatched into a colourful family of six."

"And that's where you go every year!"

"Of course, boy," boomed Blackbeard Smith. "Every summer, it's off to the West Indies to spend a month with Cocky Smart. Now there's not many retired pirates can boast they're invited by their former parrots to spend the summer holidays, I can tell you."

Sam was impressed.

"He looks very nice," he said, looking at the parrot's photograph. "Look at the way he's looking at you. That's the kind of pet *I'd* like."

Blackbeard Smith struck a match against his wooden leg and lit his pipe thoughtfully.

"And why shouldn't you?" he asked after a

while. "And why not, then? Mind, it would have to be specially worked out. Go home now, boy, and say sorry to your aunt, and come down here and see me this time tomorrow."

Sam could hardly wait. He arrived promptly at Blackbeard's shed next day and knocked on the door. Blackbeard took him into the marvellous sitting room and handed him a glass.

"Have a quick shot of this, boy," he said. "Afternoon tea."

And he winked at Sam.

Sam swallowed a large mouthful. A terrible burning seized his throat. He coughed and spat and spluttered.

"What is it?"

"Rum, boy, rum," said the old pirate. "Builds growing boys. Now if you just sit tight here I've got something next door you're going to be very pleased to see."

Sam sat down gratefully. He was feeling dizzy from the effects of the rum.

"Close your eyes," shouted Blackbeard from outside the door.

Sam's eyes were already shut. The rum had made them sting.

"Open them now!"

Sam decided he was feeling better. He opened his eyes cautiously and saw, sitting on the pirate's shoulder, a strange object covered by a tea towel.

"Pull it off, boy," growled Blackbeard Smith. Sam lifted off the tea towel.

Underneath sat a beautiful shiny metal parrot.

"Oh!" cried Sam, "*IT'S WONDERFUL.*"

"He's yours," said Blackbeard Smith.

And he lifted the parrot onto Sam's shoulder.

"Made him meself last night. Have a good close look at him now."

Sam was overjoyed.

"He's fantastic. I love him. Oh thank you, Blackbeard, thank you."

"Just take good care of him, that's all," muttered the old pirate. "Now off you go. I've got me summer holiday packing to do. Can't find me spare hook anywhere."

Sam went racing into the street, his parrot on his shoulder.

"Look, everybody, look!" he shouted. "*I've got a pet. A fantastic parrot.*"

*   *   *

Sam's parrot was a great success. He took him to school next morning.

"His name's Achilles," he told his friends at morning playtime and they all took turns at stroking the parrot.

"Where did you get him?" asked David.

"It's a secret," said Sam.

Achilles' fame spread.

After school everyone wanted to walk home with Sam and carry Achilles for him. Sam kept the parrot firmly on his own shoulder.

"He's new to me," he explained. "He has to get used to me. I can't go handing him round to everyone or he'll get frightened."

"Can I come to tea?" asked David when they got to Sam's gate.

Sam hesitated. He was longing to have David in and to show off Achilles and let him meet Blackbeard Smith. But he remembered Aunt Hilda's cross look and thought better of it.

"I'm not allowed to have people to tea," he said. "It's my aunt. She gets headaches easily."

David was disappointed.

"Well, bring Achilles out later," he said.

"And let me have *one* turn with him. I am supposed to be your best friend, after all."

Sam took Achilles out after tea and they took turns with him on their shoulders. When he got home, Sam saw Blackbeard in the garden. He and Achilles rushed down to the shed.

"Look, Blackbeard," cried Sam. "He's really good. Everybody likes him and he sits on *my* shoulder all the time and see how he looks at me. Just like Cocky Smart."

"What does your aunt say?" asked the pirate.

"*She* thinks he's just a toy. She doesn't know he's a real pet," said Sam.

"All to the good, boy," remarked Black-beard Smith. "And I shouldn't tell her meself if I were you. Now, I'm off early tomorrow morning and when I come back there'll be a present from Jamaica for you. Take care of that parrot while I'm gone."

"Oh, I will!" Sam assured him. "Have a good holiday, Blackbeard."

The pirate waved his hook and disappeared into his shed.

33

Sam took Achilles up to his room and sat him on the wooden bed-end.

"There's your perch," he said. "You can sleep there."

He smiled at Achilles.

Achilles winked at him.

Sam's eyes opened wide. He couldn't possibly have seen properly.

"Achilles," whispered Sam, "wink again."

Achilles winked.

"Go to sleep," breathed Sam.

Achilles obediently put his head under his wing.

Sam climbed into bed and fell asleep.

Next day at school he told David that Achilles could wink.

"I don't believe that." David was scornful. "He's a really good parrot but he's made of metal and he can't wink."

"He can," said Sam. "At playtime I'll show you."

But Achilles refused to wink or move his head and no one believed Sam at all.

That night, Sam put Achilles on the bed-end.

"Wink!" he ordered.

Achilles winked.

"Put your head under your wing," said Sam.

Achilles did.

"He only does it with him and me around," Sam said to himself. "And I suppose maybe he'll do it with Blackbeard Smith as well, when he's back from his holiday."

Things went well for the next few days. Quite a lot of children asked Sam to tea and they all loved Achilles.

But at the end of the week something dreadful happened.

On Friday Sam and Achilles went to bed as usual. Sam had been asleep for quite a long time when he was awoken by strange noises. He opened his eyes and peeped out from under the covers.

Achilles was sitting up on the end of the bed.

"Hallo, Sam," he said. He had a very creaky metal voice.

"*HALLO!*" replied Sam. "You can *talk*."

"I've been listening to you and learning,"

creaked Achilles. "All parrots should be able to talk. And I've been singing."

"So that's what the noises were," thought Sam.

"I'm not very good yet. I'm practising," explained Achilles. "But it's used up all my energy. I'm hungry, Sam."

Sam lifted Achilles onto his shoulder and crept down to the kitchen with him.

And it was while he was searching in the cupboard for some bread and cheese for his parrot that the dreadful thing happened.

Achilles gave a creaky squawk of joy, and Sam turned round just in time to see him eating the knobs off the cooker. As Sam watched in horror, he reached out and pecked off the door handle.

"Achilles!" cried Sam in a loud whisper. "Stop it *at once*! What are you doing?"

"Mmmmm," croaked Achilles. "Delicious. Yum, yum."

And he patted his stomach contentedly with his wing.

Sam looked at the cooker, seized Achilles and rushed back up to bed as fast as he could.

Next morning there was an awful commotion.

"But how could it have happened?" asked Uncle George.

"I keep telling you I don't know, but you don't hear me." Aunt Hilda was exasperated. "What I can tell you is that it *has* happened and I can't use the cooker any more."

That night, as Sam lay in bed after his Chinese takeaway supper, he heard scuffling and creaking from the end of the bed. Sitting up, he saw Achilles climb off the bed and creep across the floor and out of the door.

Sam followed him. Somehow he thought Achilles seemed bigger and fatter. The parrot waddled into the kitchen and over to the washing machine, opened his beak, and snap, snap, he swallowed the washing machine buttons.

Sam was horrified.

"Come *here*, Achilles," he whispered.

Achilles came creaking over to him.

"You're not to eat up anything in this kitchen," said Sam. "We need all the buttons and knobs and things. Please, Achilles."

Achilles dreamily lifted the cheese grater off its hook with his wing and swallowed it down.

"But I was hungry," he croaked.

Sam gave a sigh, picked him up and went back to bed.

When he woke up next morning, he took Achilles onto his shoulder. The parrot was definitely heavier and taller than he had been the day before.

"Achilles," said Sam, "all this food is making you grow. You'll be too big to sit on my shoulder if you go on eating. You've got to stop."

That night, after his Indian takeaway supper, he measured Achilles. He was five centimetres taller!

"Achilles," said Sam sternly, "*You are not to go down to the kitchen tonight and steal things. Do you promise?*"

Achilles put his wing on his heart.

"I promise."

Sam was woken next morning by loud shouts of dismay from his uncle and aunt's room.

"All the taps in the bathroom are missing," shouted his uncle.

"*And* the cabinet doorknobs," sobbed his aunt.

"I can't have a bath!" roared Uncle George.

"This house is haunted," wept Aunt Hilda.

Sam looked at Achilles.

Achilles was even bigger.

"You *promised*," he said.

"I know," squawked Achilles, "and I was very good. I was starving but I didn't go *near* the kitchen even though the cabinet door-knobs there are much bigger."

Sam put his head in his hands. He wished Blackbeard Smith would come back soon.

Achilles wiggled his metal feathers and stroked Sam's cheek with his beak.

"I love you, Sam," he creaked.

"I know," said Sam sadly.

All day in school he couldn't concentrate. He had left Achilles hidden under the bed. Achilles was getting so much bigger, Sam couldn't carry him anywhere on his shoulder any more.

What could he do?

And Blackbeard Smith was still on holiday.

"Maybe," thought Sam, "he'll have arrived home when I get back from school today."

But as soon as he turned into his own street, he saw that something bad had happened. His uncle was standing by the gate, looking thunderous, talking to a large policeman. Sam's heart sank.

"What's happened?" he asked nervously.

"I don't know," said his uncle, "but I intend to find out. Now someone's taken the lawn-mower."

Sam knew exactly who that would be. "But it was locked in the shed," he said.

"That's right," said his uncle. "And it's too big to get out through the window."

Sam raced into the house and upstairs. Achilles was lying under the bed.

"Come out, *at once*," he cried.

Achilles wriggled out from under. He was at least twenty centimetres taller.

"Achilles!" shouted Sam. "*You* ate that lawnmower."

Achilles hung his head. His beak trembled.

"I know," he whispered. "I was terribly hungry."

Sam was distraught.

"Oh, Achilles, what shall I *do* with you?"

"I don't know," said Achilles humbly. "I get so hungry I can't help myself. That lawn-mower was delicious. I won't need to eat again for ages."

Sam looked at him.

"If you eat any more," he warned, "you won't be able to fit under my bed and you'll have to stay outside."

An oily tear trickled down Achilles' face.

"I don't want to stay outside by myself."

"Well, *stop eating*."

Sam picked up his football.

"I'm going out and you're not coming with

me," he said. "You're staying inside. You're getting too big for my shoulder."

But Achilles looked so sad that Sam felt sorry for him and decided to carry him into the garden and hide him behind the shed while he went off to play football.

He and his friends had been playing for about an hour when they heard a lot of noise and saw an odd procession of people coming towards the park.

At the front was a very fat, very angry woman with a small boy crying loudly beside her, and behind them came three more children, two boys on bicycles, two mothers, three fathers, a tramp, a policeman, Sam's uncle, another half dozen children, four dogs and a big tom cat. And right at the back, Sam saw, with a sinking heart, a strangely familiar figure wrapped in a large old gardening coat and cap. It was Achilles. He had gone out by himself for the first time.

The procession came into the park. The very fat woman was shouting angrily and waving her fists. Sam went up to her.

"What's the matter?" he asked.

"Matter!" shouted the woman. "I'll tell you what's the matter. Somebody's stolen his tricycle! That's what's the matter. We're all looking for the thief and when we catch him, I'll make him sorry, I can tell you."

Sam seized his football and joined the procession behind Achilles.

As soon as he could he pulled the parrot to one side.

"I was just helping them look," said Achilles.

Sam was angry. "You're telling me a lie. *You* ate that tricycle."

Achilles was embarrassed.

"How did you know?"

"Look at yourself, you stupid parrot!" shouted Sam.

"I'm not a stupid parrot," sobbed Achilles. "You said I was fantastic. And I'm so hungry."

"Well, you're not a fantastic parrot now. You're an enormous parrot with tricycle wheels coming out of your shoulders," cried Sam in despair. "I don't know what to feed you with, and I can't keep people from knowing it's you doing all these things for much longer."

"You don't love me any more," wept Achilles. "Just because I'm hungry and I've got too big. I don't mean to eat things. But they look so delicious and I'm always starving. Please help me, Sam."

"I don't know how to help you," said Sam.

"But you're clever," said Achilles. "You can read and add up."

"We'd better go home," said Sam, "and see if Blackbeard Smith's back from his holiday.

Maybe he can suggest something."

But Blackbeard Smith was still away.

"You'll have to go in the tool shed," said Sam. "Wait here and I'll get the key. I'm sorry, Achilles, but I daren't risk taking you inside."

For Achilles was now taller than Sam.

"I'm scared of the dark," moaned Achilles.

"I'll bring you my torch," said Sam, "and tomorrow I'll try to think of something."

By the time Sam got back with the key and the torch, Achilles had eaten the incinerator and was another fifteen centimetres taller.

"Kiss me good night," begged the parrot.

"I can't reach your beak," said Sam.

With a lot of creaks and clangs, Achilles bent down. Sam kissed his beak and went inside to bed.

He tossed and turned all night long and slept very badly.

Next day he decided not to go to school.

"I've got a sore throat," he told his aunt.

"Measles, I expect," she said. "Well, I'm going out this morning. You'll have to stay here by yourself."

Sam was overjoyed. It would make it much

simpler to get the parrot out of the garden.

But where could he put Achilles? He went out to the tool shed as soon as his aunt had left.

Achilles was delighted to see him and stroked Sam's head with his metal wing.

"You've thought of something?" he creaked hopefully.

"Not exactly. I'm just sorting something out," said Sam untruthfully. "First, we have to get you out of the garden."

He draped the coat round Achilles and pulled the cap low down over his beak, then together they set off along the street. Sam had no idea where he was going, but headed vaguely in the direction of the park. Then, ahead of them, Sam saw a policeman. Quick as a flash, he pulled Achilles down onto a low brick wall and sat beside him.

"Keep your head down," he hissed.

The policeman stopped and looked at them with mild interest.

"Good morning," he said.

"Good morning," creaked Achilles.

"It's my grandpa," said Sam. "He's got a

bad chest."

"What a shame," said the policeman, and walked on.

Then, as Sam sat racking his brains, he had a sudden wonderful idea.

"Get up quickly, Achilles, we're going to the park."

They got to the park and Sam looked cautiously round for a suitable spot.

"Over there," he decided.

He took Achilles to an empty space among the trees, pulled off the coat and told the parrot to take off the cap.

"Now, just stand here," ordered Sam.

"But everyone will see me," objected Achilles.

"*Exactly!*" said Sam. "They'll think you're a park statue. You'll be quite safe and I can go away and try to sort out something. But you must promise to stay right here."

"I promise."

"And you won't move away?"

"No."

"Good," said Sam. "I'll be back in about an hour."

And he set off to find a solution.

He wandered round the streets for a long time trying to think of something, but by the time he returned to the park he still had no idea what to do about Achilles.

As he got near the open space where he had left the parrot, he saw a crowd had gathered. Feeling uneasy, he pushed his way through.

Achilles was still standing where Sam had left him, but he had clearly been away. Out of his head gushed a bright jet of water. As soon as Sam had gone, he had eaten the park fountain!

"That statue wasn't there yesterday," insisted a woman at the front of the crowd.

"Don't move," hissed Sam to Achilles. "Stand still."

"I *am* standing still," said the man next to Sam.

The crowd continued to argue about the new statue. Things were becoming heated when there was a sudden shout from behind them.

"Look out! Look out! Danger!"

"It's the electronic mechanical digger," shouted another voice. "It's out of control and it's heading this way!"

The crowd of people scattered in all directions.

Sam looked at Achilles.

"Hoist me up!" he ordered. "Hurry!"

Achilles lifted Sam in his beak and set him on his shoulder.

The digger was advancing quickly. You could see where it had been by the trail it was cutting through the park. As Sam watched, it tore down the park gates, and veered off along the street, ripping up large chunks of the road as it went. People ran screaming away from it.

"What is it?" asked Achilles.

" A digger," said Sam, "and its electronic brain's gone wrong."

"It looks *delicious*," said Achilles. "And I'm starving again."

And with Sam clinging to his neck feathers, he lumbered off after the huge machine.

But as they raced along, Sam realized in horror that the digger was heading towards his own street.

Achilles, who was getting hungrier and hungrier, ran faster and faster.

"I wish that pirate had made me with longer wings and I could fly," he panted.

They drew closer. Sam saw that the digger had begun to swerve and was tearing up the fence round his aunt and uncle's garden.

Aunt Hilda leant out of the top-floor window, shouting and screaming.

"Help, help! I'll be killed! It's coming straight for me. Oh help, someone!"

The digger dug up the rose garden. It was coming towards the house.

"Hurry, Achilles!" cried Sam.

Achilles leapt forward on his enormous feet. He opened his great beak.

CRUNCH!

He bit off the digger's metal jaws.

CRUNCH! CRUNCH!

He bit off the digger's mechanical arm.

CRUNCH! CRUNCH! CRUNCH!

He gobbled up the digger's caterpillar tracks and half of the empty cab.

And while Aunt Hilda watched in astonishment, he chewed up all the rest of it.

The mechanical digger was completely eaten up.

"Sam," said Achilles, "that was the best meal I've had yet. I'll have to sit down to digest it."

Aunt Hilda threw open the window.

"Is that you, Sam?" she called.

Sam's heart sank.

"Yes," he whispered.

"You wonderful, clever, amazing boy," cried Aunt Hilda. "You've saved my life!"

She rushed out of the door and ran across the garden.

"Oh, Sam, how can I ever thank you enough," she said. "You're to choose anything you want, anything at all."

And just at that moment, there came the sound of a familiar voice.

"Is anybody at home to greet the Terror of the Tearing Tea-clippers?" it shouted. "Come out, or I'll carve ye up with me hook."

And there, behind Sam, appeared Blackbeard Smith. He looked down at Achilles who was fast asleep after his enormous meal.

"Having a little trouble, are we?" he enquired genially. "Something gone a little bit wrong somewhere has it, then?"

And taking an oil-can in his hook, he dripped three drops onto Achilles' tail feathers, adjusted a knob somewhere in Achilles' chest and turned a screw in his head feathers.

There was a clanging and grinding and a sudden rushing clunk and Achilles shrank back to his old size.

"Oh, Blackbeard," said Sam. "He's normal again. He's fixed."

"Quite himself, I can tell ye," said the pirate. "Been eating, has he?"

"Everything," Sam said. "Just everything. And there was nothing I could do."

He bent down and picked up Achilles in his arms.

"He's cured now," said Blackbeard Smith. "It won't happen again, ye may be sure."

At that moment Aunt Hilda, who had been inspecting the damaged fence, noticed the pirate.

"Mr Smith," she said, with a warm smile. "How was your holiday? I'm delighted to see you back. We do miss your services in the garden, you know."

Blackbeard Smith looked hard at Sam.

"This brave boy," continued Aunt Hilda, "has just saved me from a frightful death. I was lying down with a headache when I heard a terrible noise and saw that dreadful machine coming straight at the house."

"Cured your headache, ma'am, without a doubt," said Blackbeard Smith.

"I shall never have a headache again," said Aunt Hilda. "And Sam is to choose anything he wants as a reward."

"Anything?" asked Sam.

"Anything," said his aunt.

"Choose careful now, boy," said the pirate.

"Well," said Sam, thinking hard, "first, I'd like to be allowed friends to tea; and friends *I* choose."

"Of course," said Aunt Hilda.

"Then," Sam went on, "I want to be allowed to go into Blackbeard Smith's shed any time he says I can."

"Certainly," said Aunt Hilda.

"And, last of all, I'd like to be allowed as many pets as I want."

Aunt Hilda swallowed hard.

"Well…" she said.

"You promised," said Sam.

"Yes," said Aunt Hilda, "I did. And you can. I shall speak to Uncle George about it tonight."

"Very lucky that. Nice piece of timing there," said Blackbeard Smith. "Because it just so happens I brought the young hero a little present from Jamaica."

And he pulled a box out of his coat pocket.

Sam opened the box. Inside was a tortoise.

"Oh, Blackbeard!" cried Sam, "I've always wanted a tortoise."

"And one or two other things," said the pirate, "which we'll deal with later. Meanwhile here's a shell which sings if you hold it to your ear."

"It is a rather beautiful tortoise," said Aunt Hilda. "I feel I could probably get to like it in time. But perhaps we should go inside now and have some tea."

"Aunt Hilda," said Sam, "I've decided to ask someone to tea today."

"Today?"

"Yes, today. I want Blackbeard Smith to come to tea."

"Of course, dear," said his aunt. "Mr Smith will be very welcome."

They went into the kitchen and sat down at the table.

"As it's such a special day today," said Aunt Hilda, "and you have a friend to tea, I've decided to go out and buy ice-cream and cake."

"Oh, thank you," cried Sam, and he gave Aunt Hilda a kiss.

Aunt Hilda was pleased. She took her purse and went out.

Blackbeard Smith and Sam were left alone together. Achilles was still asleep on Sam's shoulder. Sam's tortoise was sitting on his knee.

"It's been a busy time, I see," remarked the retired pirate.

"I've been waiting every day for you to come back," said Sam.

"Sorry ye've had so much trouble with him, boy," said the pirate. "But he's all right now."

"Blackbeard," said Sam, "have you ever owned a dog?"

"Dog?" The pirate looked interested. "Of

course I've had a dog. A sea-faring dog that was tied to the mast in the storms of the Indian Ocean. There's nothing about dogs Blackbeard Smith don't know. Remarkable dog I had, and many's the time Cocky Smart rode on his back."

"If I had a dog, do you think I could train Achilles to ride on its back?"

"Undeniably, boy. That bird can be trained to do anything."

"When I get my dog," asked Sam, "will you show me how to train him?"

Blackbeard rested his hook on Sam's shoulder. "Without a doubt, boy. Without a doubt. We'll begin discussing it right away."

And they were still discussing it when Aunt Hilda came back with the ice-cream and cake, a bottle of rum for Blackbeard Smith, and a packet of birdseed for Achilles.

"A kind thought, ma'am," said the pirate, "but that bird don't touch birdseed. A few drops of 3-in-1 oil will do him fine."

Achilles opened his eyes and looked around hungrily.

Aunt Hilda went to the cupboard under the

sink, took out the bicycle oil, put a little in her saucer and gave it to him.

Achilles looked at Sam.

"*Can I?*"

Sam looked at Blackbeard Smith.

"Can he?"

"Of course he can," said the pirate. "Cocky Smart's favourite tipple is marshmallow-flavoured coconut oil."

Achilles dipped his beak into the saucer and gave a deep sigh of contentment.

"You know something?" Sam said to Black-beard and Aunt Hilda. "However many pets I get, my favourite will always be Achilles."

And Achilles snuggled comfortably into Sam's neck and lovingly pecked his ear.

ARSÍNO-EE AND THE GREBBLE

One day appeared upon the roads
Of sleepy Hertfordshire
A monstrous thing that breathed out smoke
And set the towns on fire.

It made its scaly lumbrous way
Across each field and wood
And burnt down crops and trees and barns
And houses where they stood.

It swallowed cows and stable boys
And hens and pigs for food
And every little child it met
It gobbled up and chewed.

It burned down Bushey, Radlett, Mimms,
It chewed up Brookmans Park,
Then headed off across the fields
To Swipping-in-the-Nark.

Now Swipping, as you're sure to know,
Is very, very small.
It only has five shops, a church,
A pub and village hall.

And when the Swipping villagers
Were told by Scotland Yard
The grebble was approaching them,
They took it very hard.

"Our church is mediaeval,"
Sighed the Reverend Cuthbert Stone.
"Imagine if it eats the font!"
He gave a hollow moan.

Miss Gilbertson, the postmistress,
Who kept the general store
Was told the news and fainted
Dead away upon the floor.

"I'm sorry," said Inspector Grey,
"The news is rather sad.
It's certainly approaching here
And things look very bad."

"But surely, sir," cried Dr Brown,
"The Yard will stop this pillage.
You cannot let this ugly thing
Destroy our pretty village."

"I'm sorry," the inspector said,
"But what I've said is true.
The grebble is a frightful beast:
There's nothing we can do."

The villagers were so dismayed
That, in the village square,
They called a meeting. Everyone
For miles around was there.

"Has anyone a plan at all?"
The Reverend Cuthbert cried.
"We must destroy this fearful beast!"
But nobody replied.

There was a most unusual child,
By name, Arsíno-ee.
She said, "It's time that awful thing
Came face to face with *me*."

Arsíno-ee was round and fair,
Her eyes were small and pink:
She had a very clever brain.
She switched it on to THINK.

"I think," said sweet Arsíno-ee,
"I have a clever plan.
I think that I will trap that beast
I'm certain that I can."

"You couldn't, dear. You're just a child,"
The village doctor said.
Arsíno-ee replied with heat,
"You go and boil your head!

You're far too old: your brain's worn out.
You leave this job to me."
The villagers, aghast, replied,
"Just let her wait and see.

The grebble's bound to eat her up
And, as she is so rude,
It serves her right if she ends up
As gobbled grebble food."

But one of them cried, "Let her try!
Her eyes are small and pink,
And everybody knows that that
Will mean that she can think."

Arsíno–ee went home and got
Some marbles, rope and ham,
Her capgun, soap, a loaf of bread,
And bubblegum and jam.

She stretched the rope beneath some trees,
Spread marbles on the ground,
Put down the soap and laid the food
Together in a mound.

A sudden rumble sounded near,
The birds flew off in fright,
The trees and buildings bent and shook.
THE GREBBLE CAME IN SIGHT!

Arsíno-ee was not afraid.
She stood out in the square
And shouted, "Hey, you ugly beast!
Arsíno-ee is here!"

The grebble roared a mighty roar,
Arsíno-ee stood calm.
"I'll eat you up!" the monster screamed.
Arsíno-ee said, "Garn!

"You couldn't eat a rotten egg,
You couldn't fight a flea,
And even if YOU think you're wild
You simply don't scare me."

The grebble reared its ugly head
And fixed her with its eye.
Arsíno-ee looked bravely back,
And all she said was, "Hi!"

The monster rushed towards the girl,
(She stood beside the bread),
It lumbered onwards, breathing fire,
Then smelt the food ahead.

"Ah! *Bread and jam!*" the grebble cried.
"My very favourite food!
I'll have you for the second course,
Although it's rather rude."

It made a dash towards the food
But slipped upon the soap,
Then on the marbles slid about
And tripped across the rope.

It lay there on the village street,
Arsíno–ee came by.
She blew a bubble from her gum
And glued the grebble's eye.

"Help! Help!" the monster cried in fright.
"It's gone as dark as night."
Arsíno–ee took out the rope
And tied the grebble tight.

She held her capgun in her hand
And stood beside its head.
"Look out!" she said. "I've got a gun:
I'm going to shoot you dead."

"No! No!" the grebble sobbed in fear,
"I'm sorry I was bad.
I had no bread and jam to eat
I went a little mad."

"You're very bad. I ought to shoot.
I really think I should."
The grebble cried, "Arsíno-ee,
I promise to be good.

Don't shoot me please. I won't be bad
I really will be good.
I'll clean your house and make your tea
And carry coal and wood."

Arsíno–ee thought long and hard.
She said, "It seems a shame.
At least I ought to let you try.
Perhaps you weren't to blame.

I'll take you home and try it out.
You'll have to be polite,
And clean the house and give me rides
And stay inside at night."

"I will! I will!" the grebble cried.
"I'll carry you around."
Arsíno–ee climbed on its back.
It got up off the ground.

Along the village street they went;
She gave a mighty shout.
"I've stopped the grebble. Now it's safe
Come on, you cowards, come out!"

The villagers were all amazed.
"You clever thing!" they said.
"I've got pink eyes," the girl replied.
"I really use my head.

I'm going to take this monster home.
(We're just in time for tea.)
Next time you need a problem solved
You'd better send for me."

The grebble is in Swipping still,
It's with Arsíno-ee.
It never roars or breathes out fire
Or makes the people flee.

It likes to help Arsíno-ee
In every way it can
And, in return, she always feeds it
Lots of bread and jam.

GEORGIANA AND THE DRAGON

Once upon a time in a far country, there lived a king in a golden palace. The palace had television in every room, a soda fountain in the billiard room, and in the throne room was an ice-cream-making machine which could produce one-hundred and forty-seven different flavoured ice-creams. All the waterfalls in the palace gardens were made of lemonade and the mud at the edges was chocolate.

The king had one child, the Princess Georgiana. She had red hair and green eyes and a very hot temper, and she loved playing football and doing daring unusual things, whenever she could find any to do.

The king should have been very happy, but he had one serious problem. His kingdom was being terrorized by a huge dragon which had suddenly flown in a year before and had settled in a cave on the top of a hill thirteen miles from the palace. The king knew the cave very well indeed because he had a treasure hoard hidden there just in case he should ever need it, and now the dragon was in the cave guarding the treasure and making it impossible for the king to get it back.

"The whole situation's hopeless," sighed the king to his Lord Chamberlain.

"It does seem so, Your Majesty," agreed the Lord Chamberlain.

"And," went on the king, "as if that's not bad enough, the wretched monster has taken to going out from time to time and breathing on the crops and forests and burning them up. Three of the peasants have lost their houses as well. Everybody's getting very fed up and they're all expecting *me* to do something about it."

"Well, you *are* the king. It's only natural they should look to you for help," said the

Lord Chamberlain.

"I don't see that." The king was annoyed. "It's not my responsibility."

The Lord Chamberlain was firm.

"Well, the people think it is, Your Majesty. And if Your Majesty wants to keep their loyalty and support, and remain a much-loved monarch…"

"All right, all right," muttered the king. "So what do I do about it?"

"With respect…" began the Lord Chamberlain.

"Forget the respect," said the king testily. "And get on with the ideas. And quickly."

The Lord Chamberlain quietly ground his teeth together and went on.

"As I was saying, what Your Majesty needs is a contest."

"A contest?"

"To find a prince to kill the dragon and free the people from their worries about it and the bonfires it creates, and also to release Your Majesty's treasure."

"It's a good idea in theory," said the king, "but in practice, I can't think of any princes, or even knights, come to that, who'd be crazy enough to do it. That dragon breathes fire."

"Exactly," said the Lord Chamberlain, "which is why Your Majesty is offering a large reward. It's called an incentive," he explained.

"But I'm not offering one," said the king, puzzled.

"You must, Your Majesty," said the Lord Chamberlain. "Or none of them will agree to try to kill the dragon."

"What shall I offer?" asked the king.

"In these cases," said the Lord Chamberlain, "it's usual to offer the hand of the Princess in marriage and half your kingdom."

"HALF MY KINGDOM!" The king was outraged. "That's insane."

"But necessary," said the Lord Chamberlain.

"A quarter then," said the king sulkily.

"No, a quarter's too little," said the Lord Chamberlain. "Perhaps a third now and the rest when Your Majesty is no longer with us. Which, of course, we hope will not be for many, many years yet," he added hastily, noticing the king's expression.

"Well, as you say I've got no choice," said

the king, "I'll obviously have to do it. But I don't like it, I can tell you."

"Since Your Majesty's mind is now made up, I'll go off and draw up a set of rules for the contest and broadcast the news of the competition," said the Lord Chamberlain.

And he rushed off before the king could change his mind.

The king went moodily over to the ice-cream machine and ordered himself a treble bubblegum, wild strawberry and Chinese king prawn ice-cream with a giant flake. Some time later, as he was finishing it, the Lord Chamberlain came back.

"I've drawn up the rules," he announced, "and I've posted notices of the contest all over the palace, and sent messengers off to all four corners of the kingdom to put up notices and spread the word."

"How long will that take?" asked the king.

"About an hour or two," said the Lord Chamberlain. "Three, at most. They all went on trail bikes."

* * *

By nightfall, fourteen knights and three princes had registered as contestants.

"I wish there were more princes," sighed the king.

"There might be. More may apply tomorrow," said the Lord Chamberlain. "But I must remind Your Majesty that princes are in short supply. I'm surprised that as many as three have entered."

"Prince Blanziflor's on the register, I see," said the king. "I'm pleased about that. His mother's an old friend of mine. I think he should try first. If I have to give up some of my kingdom, I don't mind so much if it's Blanziflor who wins it."

"He has to slay the dragon first," reminded the Lord Chamberlain.

In the next morning's mail bag there were another five applications.

"Superb," said the king. "We shall start tomorrow."

And he ordered a large canopy to be put up and invited all the people to watch a display by the princes and knights who were going to fight the dragon.

"They can stay in the palace until it's their own turn," he explained to the Lord Chamberlain and the Court Jester, "and we will have entertainments every night for them."

The jester hurried away looking pleased. He liked showing off at entertainments.

The following afternoon the dragon slayers assembled on their horses in the palace yard. From under the canopy a large crowd watched them, impressed. In the special royal box in the centre sat the Princess Georgiana and behind her sat the rest of the palace staff. The princess looked interestedly at the competitors.

"I hope the dragon gets them all," she remarked to the Lord Chamberlain.

"Your Highness!" The Lord Chamberlain was shocked.

"Well, I don't want to marry any of *them*," said the princess. "I don't even think much of their horses."

There was a scuffle at the portcullis. It was raised. The king peered out.

"Who is it?"

"It's me," said a voice, and in on a large white horse rode a rather scruffy-looking prince in a football shirt.

"Prince Blanziflor, Your Majesty," he announced to the king, jumping off his horse and bowing low. A large guitar case was strapped to the back of his saddle.

"I got lost," he explained. "I'm sorry I'm late."

"You're just in time," said the king. "I know your mother. How is she?"

"Rather upset, I'm afraid," said Blanziflor. "She's very worried that I'll be eaten by the dragon. I *am* her only son, you see. But, on the other hand, times are hard and there aren't many other kingdoms going begging at present, and it did seem a good opportunity…"

"Quite," said the king. "Naturally. Of course. Well," he went on, ushering Prince Blanziflor into the courtyard, "you're here now, and that's what counts."

"I say," said Prince Blanziflor, looking up. "Is that the princess? She looks nice." And he waved.

Princess Georgiana waved back.

"Who's that?" she asked the Lord Chamberlain.

"Prince Blanziflor, I think," said the Lord

Chamberlain.

"I hope the dragon doesn't eat *him*," said the princess.

The dragon-slayers' pageant began. The crowds cheered and applauded as the young princes and knights rode up and down the courtyard in their armour. When it was finally over, the king lit the bonfire for the royal fireworks display. The Princess Georgiana was watching the Catherine wheels and rockets when she felt a tap on her shoulder. She turned around.

"I say," said an eager voice, "I've been trying to meet you for ages. Hello."

"Hello!" said the princess. "Who are you?"

"Prince Blanziflor."

"I'm the Princess Georgiana."

"I know," said the prince. "Can you play football?"

"I love it!" cried the princess. "If you sneak round the back with me now we could kick a few balls while no one's looking."

"Great," said the prince.

He took her hand and together they crept away from the crowd and out onto the palace football pitch. They had been practising goals for a while when the princess said, "What time is it?"

"I don't know," said the prince. "I haven't got a watch. But it's quite late."

"Oh dear," said the Princess Georgiana, "I'm supposed to be at the banquet."

"So am I," said the prince.

"But I'm the guest of honour."

"Well," said Blanziflor, "we'll just have to creep in together and hope no one notices."

They went back to the palace entrance and slipped into the banqueting hall. The king looked up from the end of the golden table.

"Where have *you* been?" he said severely.

"Oh, Papa…" began the princess, but Prince Blanziflor interrupted, "I'm terribly sorry, Your Majesty, I asked the princess to show me the palace maze and I'm afraid we got lost."

"You seem to make a habit of getting lost," said the king. "Well, now that you both *are* here, you'd better sit down and start eating."

The Princess Georgiana sat on her father's right hand. Prince Blanziflor sat near the bottom of the table.

At the end of the meal the king rose and gave a speech of welcome and thanks to all the competitors. Then he announced, "The Lord Chamberlain has drawn lots to see who will have first chance of slaying the dragon, and here is the list of princes and knights in the order they will go off to fight.

First, Prince Belvedere.

Second, the Star Green Knight.

Third…"

He droned on until the princess heard,

"Seventeenth, Prince Blanziflor."

"Maybe, by then," she thought, "the dragon will be badly wounded and Prince Blanziflor will succeed."

The banquet finished, and after drinking one another's health, everyone retired to bed.

The next day, to the accompaniment of great cheers, Prince Belvedere set off to fight the dragon.

The king's messenger returned the day after with unhappy news.

"I'm afraid, Sire, Prince Belvedere has been eaten by the dragon."

In quick succession followed four knights

and two more princes.

"Your Majesty," said the Lord Chamberlain, several days later, after the palace messenger had reported the fifteenth competitor frizzled up by dragon's breath and the sixteenth fatally wounded by dragon's claws, "is it sensible to continue?"

"As I recall," said the king, "this was *your* idea, not mine, so it's on your head, I'm afraid."

"The next contestant," cried the Court Usher, "has come to say farewell, Your Majesty. Prince Blanziflor."

The prince came jauntily into the throne room and sank on one knee.

"Your blessing, Sire," he said.

"Good luck, my boy," said the king. "And I hope you get my treasure back."

"And may I have *your* blessing, Your Highness," said Prince Blanziflor, bending low in front of the Princess Georgiana.

"Granted," replied the princess graciously. "And I have a piece of advice for you."

And she whispered in his ear, "If in doubt, give in and run."

Prince Blanziflor bowed and left.

Twelve hours later the king's messenger re-appeared.

"Terrible news, Your Majesty. Prince Blanziflor has been taken prisoner by the dragon. It's holding him hostage in the cave."

"How shocking!" cried the king. "We must send another contestant to rescue him."

"Impossible," said the Lord Chamberlain. "There were only five more competitors and they've all resigned. There's no one left to rescue him. You'll have to go yourself, Sire."

"I'd love to go, of course," said the king, "but, unfortunately, I'm too old."

"Well, I don't know what we can do, Sire," said the Lord Chamberlain.

"His mother will be awfully cross," said the king.

"Undoubtedly, Sire."

"Are you sure there are no more contestants?"

"None at all, Sire."

They sat together for some time, thinking deeply.

The door opened and the Princess Georgiana came in.

"Yes, my dear?" said the king.

"I've come to register," said the princess.

"Register?" The king was puzzled.

"For the contest."

The king looked even more puzzled. "What contest?"

"Really, Papa!" sighed the princess. "You *are* impossible. The dragon-slaying contest, of course. I want to kill the dragon."

"Georgiana!" cried the king. "Don't be so ridiculous. You can't possibly kill the dragon. I've never heard such nonsense."

"I *can* kill the dragon," said the princess calmly. "*And* rescue Prince Blanziflor. And I've come to register." She turned to the Lord Chamberlain. "Can you put my name down, please? I want to be a contestant."

"Well, you can't," said the king. "It has to be a prince who slays the dragon."

"It doesn't say so in the rules," objected the princess.

"It does," said the Lord Chamberlain.

"Where, then?" demanded the princess.

The Lord Chamberlain took up the parchment scroll. He read it through very thoroughly, then re-read it. He was on the third re-read when the king said nastily, "Well, come on, read it aloud."

The Lord Chamberlain cleared his throat.

"I can't actually find it, Your Majesty."

"See!" said the princess triumphantly.

The king looked hard at the Lord Chamberlain.

"What do you mean, you can't find it? I thought it was rule fifty-three."

"With respect, Your Majesty," mumbled the Lord Chamberlain, "rule fifty-three is to do with claims of compensation in the event of death by dragon's breath."

"I told you it wasn't in the rules," said the princess, "so I'm going."

"It's unfeminine," said the king. "No one's ever heard of a princess fighting a dragon."

"They will have after I've done it," said the princess.

The king sighed heavily.

"I wonder if commoners have these troubles," he remarked to the ceiling.

"Undoubtedly, Sire," cried the Lord Chamberlain and the Court Usher simultaneously.

"Not much consolation," said the king.

And to the princess he said, "Well, under the circumstances, I don't suppose I can stop you."

"I'll need a longbow, this list of equipment and a red suit of armour," said the princess. "Do you think someone could get them for me by morning, please? Oh, and a banner, of course."

"I'll see to it myself," said the Lord Chamberlain, and he hurried away.

"Georgiana," said the king, "let me explain it to you once more. That dragon is ferocious and desperate. It's guarding a priceless treasure and it will stop at nothing to keep it. It has Prince Blanziflor imprisoned at the back of its cave; it's already sizzled up most of the knights and princes and frightened off the rest of them. This is a doomed enterprise."

"I'm going and that's that," said the princess in an even more determined tone.

The king looked resigned.

"I've tried to stop you," he said. "I've explained the dangers and, of course, you *are* my only daughter and I love you dearly, but if you won't listen to reason and you want to upset me and cause me grief and woe, go right ahead."

"That's emotional blackmail, Papa," said the princess. "You should be ashamed of yourself. And there won't be any grief or woe: you'll be rejoicing because the dragon's slain."

"Nobody's going to slay that dragon," said the king. "How can they? It's impossible."

"I don't think so," said Georgiana, and then, with a sudden surge of enthusiasm, she asked, "Do you think, as it might be my last meal for ages, we could have passion-fruit layer cake for supper?"

"It might be your last meal ever, so I suppose we'd better," said the king moodily. "Order it from Cook. But I won't enjoy it much, I can tell you."

Princess Georgiana set off for the kitchen. On the way she met the Lord Chamberlain.

"Your Highness," began the Lord Chamberlain.

"Yes?"

"It's about your heraldic emblem. What creature would you like emblazoned on your shield? All the knights have an animal or bird or heraldic beast of some kind."

The princess thought for a bit. Then she

said, "A gerbil, I think. I like gerbils."

"I'm not sure that a gerbil is quite suitable," said the Lord Chamberlain.

"Well, it's what I want," said the princess cheerily and she sped away to the kitchen.

The princess got up next morning, dressed in her new red armour which the maid had laid out for her, and went down to breakfast. Crowds of people were assembling outside the palace to watch her set off. She collected her equipment and her sandwiches, brushed her teeth thoroughly with her golden tooth-brush, kissed the king and went outside.

The people cheered and she gave a gracious wave as she jumped into her red sports car with the golden gerbil emblem on each door and the small gold crown on top. She revved up the engine and set off. Behind her came a groom driving the royal horse-box with her horse, Bucephalus, inside.

About two miles from the dragon's cave the princess pulled up. The horse-box stopped behind her and the groom got out.

"Please get my horse ready now," said the

princess. "Look. I can see smoke on the horizon. It must be the dragon."

"I expect so, Your Highness," said the groom nervously, and he began to open the horse-box. He paused. "Your horse may not like the smoke," he pointed out.

"Bucephalus isn't frightened of *anything*. I trained him myself."

"Will Your Highness actually be needing me," asked the groom, "or will it be all right for me to go back to the palace?"

"Oh, you can go back," the princess assured him. "I can manage quite well by myself."

The groom saluted with a trembling hand. He set up the mounting steps. "Thank you, ma'am," he said with relief.

And he tied Bucephalus to a nearby tree, shut up the royal horse-box and jumped in behind the steering wheel.

Two seconds later he was out again. "Good luck, Your Highness."

"Oh thanks," said the princess and she waved to him as he drove away.

Bucephalus whinnied and lifted his head. Princess Georgiana stroked his neck.

"Good boy," she said soothingly, and she untied the reins, climbed on to the mobile steps (because she was quite heavy in her armour) and got on to his back.

"Here we go," she said to herself, and they set off to meet the dragon.

They had not gone far when the smoke began to get thicker and the air grew warmer.

"Thank goodness I had special heatproof armour made," said the princess to her horse.

They rode on. As they approached the hill where the dragon was guarding the cave, they could hear the sounds of a guitar.

"That must be Prince Blanziflor, trapped inside. I suppose that's how he passes the time," thought the princess.

Bucephalus snorted.

Flames were shooting out of the cave entrance but Princess Georgiana hummed to herself and thought contentedly of the fire extinguisher strapped to her sword case.

At the bottom of the hill she stopped, jumped down from Bucephalus's back and tied him to a large rock.

"Wait there like a good horse," she told

him, patting his nose.

Bucephalus nuzzled her.

Princess Georgiana took a deep breath and set off, on foot, up the hill to meet the dragon.

There was a rumble and a roar. The ground shook. Out of the cave poked a huge hideous dragon's head.

"What do you want?" it growled nastily.

The princess smiled. "I've come sightseeing."

"Sightseeing!" snarled the dragon. "What do you mean? Sightseeing."

"I've come to see the dragon."

"I *am* the dragon," said the dragon proudly. "I terrorize the neighbourhood round here. I've frizzled up princes and knights with my hot breath already, and I've got a prince trapped in my cave. As a matter of fact," it went on confidentially, "I'm guarding a priceless treasure in there."

"You're not!" Princess Georgiana was disbelieving.

"Oh yes, I am," said the dragon, and it spat at her. A long flame shot out of its mouth.

"Could you do that again, please?" asked

the princess.

"Why?"

"I just wondered if you could."

"Of course I can," said the dragon boastfully and it shot out another sheet of flame.

"How nice," said the princess. She undid her quiver and took out a long toasting fork and a bag of marshmallows.

"Now I'll just sit here with my fork and toast marshmallows on your breath, if you don't mind."

"I'm not doing anything special right now, so I suppose I could help," said the dragon.

They sat there for some time while the princess toasted and ate marshmallows.

"I don't believe you've really got a prince in there," said Princess Georgiana.

The dragon was annoyed. "Of course I have."

"Well, where is he then?"

"I don't let him *out*," said the dragon scornfully. "He might run away. He's my hostage. He's playing the guitar in there right now."

"I see," said the princess. "Where exactly is he?"

"Down at the back of the cave."

"Oh."

She took another marshmallow from her bag, pushed it onto her fork and held it in front of the dragon.

"Blow again, please."

The dragon was irritated. "Look here," it rumbled. "I've got better things to do than sit about all day toasting marshmallows for silly girls."

"I'm not a silly girl," said the Princess Georgiana. "I'm very clever and strong *and* I can tap-dance."

"In full armour? I don't believe it," said the dragon.

"Of course I can't tap-dance in my *armour*."

"And come to that," went on the dragon, "what are you doing in full armour anyway?

Whoever heard of anyone sightseeing in armour?"

The Princess Georgiana thought quickly. "Well, I am," she said, "so now you have heard of somebody doing it. My mother makes me wear armour. I've got a very weak chest and she thinks it will stop me from catching cold."

"She sounds a bit over-protective," said the dragon.

"She is," said the princess hastily. "But, of course, I have to do as she says."

"Quite right too," said the dragon. "People should always do as their mothers tell them."

"Do *you*?" The princess was curious.

"Of course not," said the dragon. "I'm a *dragon*. Dragons don't do as they're told."

The princess was thoughtful. "I see." Then she went on, "So it wouldn't be any use telling you to stay in that cave and not follow me to see what I'm doing when I go off in a few minutes."

"No, it would not," said the dragon. "Because I'll just follow you if I want to."

"What if I *ordered* you not to follow me?"

"I don't get ordered round by anyone, especially not girls. If I decide to follow you,

you won't be able to stop me."

"I see."

Princess Georgiana put another marsh-mallow on her fork, then quickly pulled it off and ate it untoasted.

"It's a pretty day," she remarked.

"Very," agreed the dragon.

They sat in companionable silence for some time.

"I expect your cave's rather dismal and ugly inside," said the princess.

The dragon was hurt. "As a matter of fact, it's very well decorated," it snapped. "And there's a beautiful gem collection in one corner."

The princess knew all about the gem collection: she had heard her father lamenting its loss frequently.

"Oh, really," she said.

"You don't sound very impressed," complained the dragon.

"I'm sure your gems are very pretty," said the princess, "but I don't believe you've got as many as you say. I think you're boasting."

The dragon was furious. It roared out a cloud of black smoke and stamped till the ground rumbled.

The guitar music inside the cave stopped.

"How dare you?" shouted the dragon. "You ignorant girl. I'll show you if I'm boasting or not. Go inside and have a look and see if I'm telling the truth. You owe me a big apology."

"If it's true, I'll apologize," said the princess. "And if it's not true, you have to."

"IT IS TRUE!" screamed the dragon. "Go in there and look!"

It moved to one side of the cave entrance.

The princess went cautiously forward. It was pitch black inside. She took a deep breath and stepped past the dragon, into the dark.

At first she could see nothing at all, then, as her eyes adjusted to the gloom, she noticed a faint glow at the very back of the cave. She moved towards it, and, as she drew nearer, she realized that the light was coming from an enormous heap of coloured stones.

"My goodness," breathed the princess to herself, "it must be the gem collection! But it can't be. It's enormous."

She gazed around her. Diamonds, rubies, emeralds, sapphires, turquoises, opals and bars of gold and silver sparkled and gave off a soft warm sheen.

"Amazing!" she sighed aloud.

"I know," breathed a voice beside her.

The princess jumped. "Prince Blanziflor."

She had forgotten all about him in the excitement of going into the cave.

"Ssh," he warned. "The dragon has super-acute hearing. Don't let it hear you talking to me. I've been trapped here for ages. Can you get someone to free me?"

"*I've* come to free you," whispered the princess.

"Good Heavens, it's Princess Georgiana! *You* free me?" The prince stifled a giggle. "But you're a girl!"

"I'm a princess actually," hissed Georgiana huffily, "and if you don't want to be rescued that's fine with me. Just let me know and I'll leave straight away."

"Oh no, please." The prince was humble. "I'm sorry. I don't care who rescues me, as long as I get out of here. I can only play three tunes on the guitar and I'm sick to death of them, and all that dragon gives me to eat is porridge. Can you imagine it?" he went on gloomily. "Porridge, porridge, porridge, three times a day. It's awful."

"You're lucky the dragon didn't kill you," said the princess. "Why hasn't it?"

"It thinks I'm too useful as a hostage," said the prince. "But I don't see how *you're* going to rescue me. There's no chance. The dragon's already killed all the other competitors."

"I know," said the princess. "I say, I think I might just slip a diamond in my quiver and take it with me."

"Don't, don't!" Prince Blanziflor was very agitated. "You mustn't. The last time that happened it burnt up the knight who did it in one breath. Just like a flame-thrower. It was terrible."

"How awful," whispered the princess. "But it won't know I've taken it."

"It will. It'll smell it," said the prince.

"Smell it?"

"Yes. Dragons can smell precious stones: their noses are very sensitive to gems and they can smell diamonds and rubies over fifty metres away."

"Gosh!" The princess was impressed.

"That's how it found this treasure," explained Prince Blanziflor. "It told me. It was flying by and it smelt gems and burned down the huge wooden doors at the cave entrance with its fiery breath. And it's been here ever since, guarding the hoard."

"I see," said the princess. "Well, I won't take anything now I know that." She thought for a minute. "I'd better go out soon or it'll get suspicious. But I've got a plan. If you want to be rescued you'll have to do as I say." She whispered something in his ear.

"Yes, I will," muttered Prince Blanziflor. "But be careful, won't you?"

"No," said the princess. "I won't be careful: I'll be clever. See you later. And don't forget to do *exactly* what I told you."

"All right," said Prince Blanziflor. "Good-bye."

The princess went out of the cave and stood blinking in the sunlight by the entrance.

The dragon looked at her in astonishment.

"You didn't take anything."

"Of course not," said Princess Georgiana.

"*I'm* not a thief. And I owe you an apology. That's a *wonderful* collection of jewels – the best I've ever seen."

The dragon looked proud.

"Where did you get them?" asked the princess.

"I found them," it said arrogantly. "All by myself. I smelt them as I was flying by."

"But didn't they belong to someone else?"

"They're mine now," said the dragon.

"But that's stealing."

The dragon was enraged.

"Shut up, shut up!" it shouted. "Stop accusing me. I won't listen!" And it stamped and screamed. The ground rumbled.

"Honestly, you are a baby," said the princess, unimpressed. "Do stop it. You're making earthquakes. And I want to tell you something. You've got someone in that cave, did you know?"

"Of course I know. It's a prince. He's my hostage. I told you already."

"Oh yes, so you did," said the princess. "What do you feed him?"

"Porridge," said the dragon. "It's good for him."

"Porridge!" The princess was incredulous. "Seriously?"

"Yes. Why not?" The dragon looked puzzled.

"Well, no reason why not," said the Princess Georgiana, "except I personally wouldn't waste good porridge on a hostage."

"What do you mean?"

"It seems to me," said the princess, "that it's a terrible waste of precious food to give porridge to a *hostage*. I wouldn't. But I suppose you can afford it with a gem collection like yours."

"I can't, I can't. I'm really terribly poor," moaned the dragon. "It's dreadful. I haven't *any* money at all. And I'd never sell my treasure. I thought the prince wouldn't like porridge and it'd serve him right to be made to eat it."

"Have it your own way, then. I don't care," said the princess.

"But what should I feed him? You must tell me."

"You can do as you want," said the princess,

"but if *I* had a hostage like that, I certainly wouldn't waste valuable porridge on him. I'd make him eat bacon and eggs every morning, and baked beans and sausages and tomatoes and roast potatoes and ice-cream and horrible things like that."

"But I thought he'd *like* those sorts of things. I want to make life hard for him."

The princess threw back her head and laughed and laughed.

"You are silly," she cried. "Fancy punishing someone by feeding him porridge. Have it your own way. Carry on. But I'll bet he loves porridge just like I do."

"Right!" said the dragon grimly. "No more porridge for him! From now on he gets bacon and eggs and baked beans."

"And whatever you do, don't give him water either," said the princess. "Make him drink lemonade or something sickly and gassy like that."

"All right," said the dragon. "And thank you. You're a great help."

"I try to be," said the Princess Georgiana. "And if I were you, I'd start with the ice-cream now. Just watch his face when you give it to him. He'll be really upset."

"Wonderful," said the dragon.

"Well, I'll be off to do some more sight-seeing," said the princess cheerily, and she got up. "Thank you for toasting my marsh-mallows. Maybe I'll come back and see you tomorrow."

"Yes, do that," said the dragon. "If your mother will let you."

"Bye," called the princess.

"Bye!" shouted the dragon.

The princess set off down the hill.

Next morning, she was back.

"Hello!" she called.

The dragon poked its head out of the cave.

"Oh, it's you."

"I came to ask you something."

"Well, ask me then," grumbled the dragon, "and hurry up about it."

"I told my mother about you and she asked if it's true that dragons have ugly great warts on their noses."

"Of course they don't!" snapped the dragon.

"What a rude, stupid girl you are. You can see for yourself I haven't got warts. In fact, I'm considered very handsome as dragons go."

"People think *I'm* pretty, too," said the princess.

"*I* don't," said the dragon.

The princess ignored him. "I told my mother about your gem collection," she went on. "And she said it couldn't be a very big one. Judging by what I told her, it didn't sound to her as big as the treasure that other dragon's got over at Widdock Hill."

"It's much bigger and better than his!" screeched the dragon. "How dare you say it's smaller? You're the most ignorant girl I've ever met."

"I'd sort of forgotten what your gems were like by the time I got home," said the princess, "so maybe I didn't describe them to my mother very well."

"Go inside that cave and look again!" ordered the dragon.

The princess seemed worried.

"I don't think I should."

"You must. I'm telling you to. And when

you've seen it again you can tell your mother
the truth. Why, it's seven times as big as that
gem collection old One-Eye's got at Widdock
Hill. No comparison at all."

The princess stepped reluctantly into the
cave.

Once she was inside she slipped to the back
and whispered in Prince Blanziflor's ear.

"Did it work?"

The prince nodded.

Then he whispered back, "The ice-cream
was *wonderful*."

"Just do as I say and trust me," said the
princess.

108

"I will," he promised.

Princess Georgiana went back outside.

"You're right," she said, impressed. "Your treasure *is* enormous. I'd forgotten. I'll get on back home and tell my mother right away."

"Oh, by the way," rumbled the dragon, "thank you for that advice about feeding the hostage. You should have seen his face when I gave him the ice-cream. He hated it."

"I'll bet he did," said the princess, and waving goodbye she set off down the hillside.

She spent the night camped about two miles away with Bucephalus. They built a fire together.

"My armour's getting heavy," complained the princess.

Bucephalus nodded sympathetically and they stretched out beside each other and fell asleep.

Next day, the princess got up very early. She rode Bucephalus back to the bottom of the hill and tied him to a tree, out of sight. Then she checked her armour and equipment, slung her longbow on her back and went up the hill.

A short distance from the cave she stopped.

"Come out, you stupid old dragon," she shouted. "I'm the Princess Georgiana and I've come to fight you and claim back my father's treasure. It's not yours. You stole it. You're nothing but a thief."

There was a low rumble from inside the cave. The ground shook.

The princess went several steps closer.

"You're afraid," she called. "You're too scared to come out and fight me!"

A blast of flame poured out of the cave entrance. Even from a distance the princess could feel the fire on her cheeks. She pulled down her heat-proof vizor and, taking out her sword, she clashed it against a large rock.

"You're not a dragon. You're nothing but a baby."

With a terrible howl, the dragon came roaring out.

"It's you!" it shrieked. "You wicked girl. I'll roast you alive."

A huge double jet of flame shot from its mouth.

Princess Georgiana hid behind a rock,

unstrapped her fire extinguisher, then, poking her head out, she cried, "Yah, yah, can't catch me!"

The dragon was enraged. It exhaled a mighty breath and shot out an even longer tongue of fire. Just as she felt the searing heat over her head, the princess raised the fire extinguisher and pressed the lever.

The dragon's fiery breath vanished. It coughed and choked and spat. By now it was thoroughly angry and furious.

"You won't escape *me*," it bellowed and, rising on its hind legs with its wings out-stretched, it showed its enormous talons. "I'll tear you to pieces!"

It was a terrifying sight. Georgiana felt as though she was in the middle of a nightmare.

"I must be calm and sensible," she whispered to herself, but her hands shook with fright. Trembling, she took out her catapult, spat on her hands for luck and with one deft movement popped a sharp stone in the sling and pulled it back.

The dragon came closer. Georgiana saw its hideous pointed teeth. She pulled the catapult sling tighter, took a deep breath and let fly. Twang!

The stone shot through the air and lodged straight in the dragon's forehead between the eyes. The dragon gave an ear-splitting scream. Fiery vapour came pouring out of the wound and black blood spurted out of its mouth. It writhed and tossed and shook, then fell in a heap onto the ground.

Princess Georgiana started towards it, then remembered what her old nanny had told her about dragons.

"They're very tricky things, dragons. Never let one fool you. Just when you think they're dead and done for, they jump up and catch you again."

So she went, very cautiously, just a little nearer. The dragon's eyes were closed and its body trembled.

"But I'd better be on the safe side," thought the princess.

She fumbled under her armour for her box of matches, pulled one out and struck it against her knee pads. It lit. Georgiana took a dead branch from the ground nearby and set fire to the end. Then she picked up her long-bow, set the branch in it like an arrow, took aim and fired the burning branch straight into the dragon's chest.

There was a tremendous explosion! A jet of flame shot into the air and covered the dragon. Boom! It frizzled up within a minute.

"Nanny was right then!" murmured the princess. "Dragons *do* have liquid gas instead of blood. How lucky I wasn't standing too close."

She looked over the edge of the crater in the

ground where the dragon had been. There was nothing left but a heap of soot and ashes.

"Serves you right!" said the princess sternly.

"You wicked dragon. Well, ex-dragon, I mean."

And she raced up to the cave to tell Prince Blanziflor he was free.

"You can come out," she called. "You're not a hostage any more. I've slain the dragon."

There was a little scuffling noise from the back of the cave.

"Are you sure?" whispered a frightened voice.

"Positive."

"But I just heard a most terrible explosion."

"I know. It was me frizzling up the dragon."

"Was it? I thought it was the dragon frizzling up *you*."

The prince peeped out of the entrance, saw the dragon was gone, and stood blinking in the unaccustomed sunlight.

He looked at the princess. His lips trembled, he threw his arms round her neck and burst into tears.

"My heroine! How can I ever thank you?" he sobbed.

Princess Georgiana patted him soothingly.

"Never mind," she said. "It's over now. All we have to do is get you back to your mother's kingdom."

Prince Blanziflor wept harder.

"I haven't even got a horse. Mine bolted when it saw the dragon."

"We can both ride on mine," said the princess generously. And she led him over to the tree where Bucephalus was waiting.

Blanziflor climbed up on the horse's back. Princess Georgiana was just about to get up too when suddenly she stopped.

"Wait," she cried and rushed back to the cave. She reappeared with a large piece of wood on which she wrote,

Then she propped up the sign at the cave entrance.

"We can come back later for the treasure," she said.

"We?" asked Prince Blanziflor.

"Me and the palace guards," said the princess.

The prince was disappointed. "I thought you meant me."

"Do you want to come? I thought you hated it here."

"It'd be different coming here with no dragon," said Blanziflor. "And with you."

The princess smiled at him.

Prince Blanziflor took her hand.

"Will you marry me?" asked the princess.

Prince Blanziflor looked disappointed again.

"You're supposed to get down on one knee and ask me," he pointed out.

"As a matter of fact," snapped the princess, "*you're* supposed to do the asking." And she stamped off in a huff. The prince thought for a moment. Then he slid off Bucephalus and went running after her.

"Georgiana," he said in honeyed tones, "I love you. Will you marry me?"

The princess turned round.

"*You* haven't gone down on one knee, I notice," she said acidly.

Prince Blanziflor knelt down.

The Princess Georgiana looked severely at him.

"You were *very* rude to me just now."

"Sorry," said the prince. "I was in a state of shock from the dragon and everything. And I'm still a bit blinded by the light. *Please*, Georgiana."

The princess gave a gracious smile.

"All right then, I will marry you. But…"

"Yes?"

"It can't be only you that's king later on when we have our own kingdom. You have to take equal turns with me."

"OK," agreed Blanziflor. "A year each."

"And if I make a law letting everyone have free ice-cream on Fridays, you can't change it."

"But supposing we run out of money for the ice-cream?"

"We won't. We've got the treasure."

"You're right," said the prince. "I'd forgotten the treasure."

"And you're not to be late for our wedding," said the princess.

"Never," said the prince.

"All right," said the princess. "So it's all settled."

"Yes."

"By the way, Blanziflor…"

"Yes?"

"I love you too," said the princess. "And when I get home I'm having an octuple double-strawberry-peanut-sausage-chocolate-crispy-bacon-vanilla-peach-stardust ice-cream with treble flakes from my father's ice-cream machine. I think I deserve it."

"I think you do, too," said the prince.

And he put his arm tenderly round her as they rode off together back to the palace.

THE GREBBLE
AND THE FLOOD

The grebble and Arsíno-ee
      Did everything they could
To live together happily
But things were not so good.

They realized that the problem was
Her house was very small,
They both were squashed: they couldn't move,
There was no space at all.

And, once again, the two of them
Had spent a sleepless night.
The grebble found it very cramped.
(The fit was rather tight.)

"I'll leave my tail outside the house,"
The grebble kindly said.
"And also," said Arsíno-ee,
"You'd better leave your head."

"Oh dear!" the grebble cried, "I simply
Can't stay in this place."
"What nonsense!" said Arsíno–ee,
"We'll have to make more space."

She set off to the village store
But everywhere she walked,
The village people looked away
And no one smiled or talked.

She bought some nails, she bought some wood,
She went to get a saw.
The villagers were gathered
In a group outside the door.

"Arsíno-ee," said Dr Brown,
"We've got to have a word.
You cannot keep the grebble here.
The idea's quite absurd.

We're grateful. You're a clever child.
You saved us all, we know.
But that's a very dangerous beast.
Your grebble has to go."

"I'm sorry," said Arsíno-ee,
And firmly set her jaw,
"The grebble stays and lives with me.
I'm saying nothing more."

"It's dangerous," the doctor said,
"There isn't any doubt.
And if you won't co-operate,
We're going to drive it out."

Arsíno-ee was very cross.
Her eyes went brightest pink.
"You'd better watch your step," she said.
"I'm going off to THINK."

And, as she walked and tried to think
Of what to do, she saw
The grebble creeping down the road,
A suitcase in its claw.

"Oh Grebble," cried Arsíno-ee,
"What are you going to do?"
"I'm leaving," sobbed the grebble,
"So they won't be cross with you."

"You mustn't!" said Arsíno-ee.
"You're staying here with me.
I'll work it out and find a plan.
Don't cry. Just wait and see."

They had their supper, went to bed,
And, some time in the night,
A storm began with pouring rain.
They woke up in a fright.

"My tail's all wet!" the grebble cried.
"There's water all around.
It's rained so hard it's made
Enormous puddles on the ground."

The morning came: the sun shone down,
But everything in Swipping –
The houses, people, cats and dogs –
Was flooded out and dripping.

Arsíno-ee was greatly pleased.
"Get up, sweet beast," she said.
"The answer to our problem's come
While we were both in bed."

"Arsíno–ee," the grebble said,
"I really can't see how."
"They need your breath," the girl replied,
"To dry the village now.

You'll have to breathe out fire and smoke
And really look ferocious."
The grebble said, "You told me
Such behaviour was atrocious.

I *used* to be a wicked beast
But now I'm very good.
I'd like to use my fire to help
But I don't think I could."

Arsíno–ee was quite annoyed.
She hit the grebble's head.
"Watch out!" she cried. "I'm going to take
Away your jam and bread."

The grebble gave a mighty roar.
It shot out flames and heat
And dried the raging torrent
That was pouring down the street.

The steam rose up. The grebble
Gave the door a mighty slam,
And, breathing fire, set off at once
In search of bread and jam.

Arsíno-ee was very quick.
She snatched up jam and bread
And crept along unnoticed
With the grebble just ahead.

The villagers were standing round
In rubber boots and macs.
They'd tried to keep the water out
By putting sand in sacks.

"But all our sacks have burst," they groaned
And some began to cry.
"Our houses, clothes and shops are soaked!
How will we get things dry?"

Just then they heard a splashing sound
And slowly, looking mean,
The grebble through the water came
Towards the village green.

"I want some bread and jam!" it shrieked.
"I WANT SOME JAM AND BREAD!"
Behind it swam Arsíno-ee
A bag perched on her head.

The grebble blew out tongues of flame
And gave a frightening scream.
The water in the village street
Dried up and turned to steam.

"Oh look!" the people called, amazed.
"The water's almost dried.
Bring out the clothes and mattresses
And everything inside."

They hung things from the windowsills
And hauled the rest outside
And every time the grebble roared
A little more got dried.

Arsíno-ee had slipped upstairs
And held the jam and bread
Just out of reach but well in view
Above the grebble's head.

The grebble turned towards the food,
Its tail swung swiftly round
And swept away the dried-up mud
That lay along the ground.

"Arsíno-ee!" the grebble roared.
"I thought you were my friend."
"I am," she sighed. "I'm helping you.
You'll see that in the end."

"If you're my friend," the grebble asked,
"Why won't you give me food?"
"I would have," said Arsíno-ee,
"But you were very rude.

You slammed the door and lumbered off.
You didn't wait to see.
But, even so, I'm still your friend,
I've brought your food with me."

The monster blushed a purple-pink
And sadly hung its head.
"Arsíno–ee, I just forgot,
I'm sorry now," it said.

And suddenly, behind them, came
The noise of many feet.
The people, bringing presents, rushed
Along the village street.

"You've got to stay! We need you here!
We'll fix your house!" they cried.
"We think that you're a hero now!"
Arsíno–ee grinned wide.

The villagers set off with wood
And hammers, nails and saws.
They raised the roof, enlarged the walls,
And put in bigger doors.

"It's wonderful," the grebble said,
"To know they all want me.
I couldn't bear to live alone
Without Arsíno–ee."

Arsíno–ee looked very smart.
"I said you needn't fear.
I *knew* that what we needed
Was a grebble living here.

Now thanks a lot and home you go.
It's late and getting dark.
You needn't fear. *We're* looking after
Swipping–on–the–Nark."

VIOLET KATZ AND THE PINK ELEPHANT

One morning Violet Katz woke up and saw a pink elephant looking in at her window.

"Ma," shrieked Violet Katz, "there's a pink elephant outside my window!"

Downstairs Mrs Katz was stirring the porridge.

"Don't be ridiculous, Violet," she shouted upstairs.

"Pa," bellowed Violet Katz, "there's a pink elephant outside my window!"

Mr Katz was taking his morning bath. He blew the soapsuds into a bubble.

"Don't be so silly, Violet. It's too early in the morning for a joke."

"Well," said Violet Katz to herself, "if they don't want to believe me that's their bad luck."

And she got up and opened the window. The elephant put its pink trunk into her bedroom, picked her up and lifted her outside and onto its back.

Violet Katz gave an encouraging elephant call and they were off.

Mrs Katz looked out of the kitchen window. She dropped the porridge spoon in surprise.

"Pa, Pa, come quick! Violet has just ridden off on the back of a large pink elephant."

Mr Katz jumped out of his bath and rushed

downstairs and out of the front door.

"Come back! Come back!" he called.

But Violet Katz and the pink elephant were far away in the distance.

A large policeman came round the corner.

"Help me, please," begged Mr Katz. "My daughter's just ridden off on the back of a large pink elephant."

"Excuse me, sir," said the policeman, "but you haven't got any clothes on and you're not allowed to walk around the streets like that."

Mr Katz looked at himself. He thought quickly.

"I have got clothes on," he said. "They're made of a very new material – gossamer foam. Many uninformed people mistake them for soapsuds."

"Well, if I were you, sir, I'd go back and change them for something more conventional," said the policeman.

Mr Katz went home.

"Did you find her?" asked Mrs Katz tearfully.

"No, I did not," said Mr Katz, "*and* I'm lucky I wasn't arrested. Now, as she's not here and she clearly won't be back for ages, I'm having her porridge as well as my own."

Violet Katz and the pink elephant were heading towards the ocean.

"Would you enjoy a day by the sea?" enquired the elephant.

"I'd love it," cried Violet Katz, and she let go of the elephant's neck as she rode along. "Look, no hands!"

"I can do trunkstands," said the elephant proudly, and he lifted Violet down and set her on the ground. "Look at me."

"That's brilliant," said Violet, impressed.

"I know," said the elephant. "That's why I'm pink. I'm always blushing with pride about how clever I am."

He put her up on his back again.

"I'm clever too," said Violet. "I can sing and whistle and dance."

"Remarkably smart," said the elephant. "Can you charge?"

"Well, no," admitted Violet, "I can't charge, but I am *extremely* good at throwing a tantrum."

"Really. I've never seen a tantrum. What is it?"

"A very bad fit of temper," explained Violet. The elephant was curious.

"Could you throw one now?"

"Not now," said Violet. "I think I'll save it up for later just in case I need it."

They had been going for some time when suddenly the elephant said, "I can see the sea!"

"Where?"

"There, in front of us."

Violet Katz looked over the elephant's ear and saw way ahead in the distance the thin blue line of the ocean.

"Faster! Faster!" she cried.

The elephant's pink ears flapped out behind him as he raced along.

"Oh, Violet Katz," he called, "I love the sea."

They raced onto the soft brown sand and sighed with pleasure at having arrived.

"Oh dear," said Violet, "I've just remembered. I haven't got a swimming costume. I'm still in my nightie."

The elephant looked thoughtful.

"I think we can work out something," he said.

"Well, what?" demanded Violet. "Here I am at the seaside in my nightie. People are going to stare at me and laugh."

"*I'm* not laughing."

"You don't count," said Violet very rudely.

The elephant was hurt.

"I'm not going to help you if you aren't kind to me," he said.

"I can't be kind when I'm worried," said Violet. "And I'm worried about not having proper clothes."

"All right," said the elephant. "I've got an idea. I'll put you down in the sand and cover you up to your neck, and you can wait for me while I get some clothes for you."

He scooped up sand with his trunk and carefully buried her.

"I'll be back soon," he promised.

And away he went.

Ten minutes later he was back with a beautiful frog-green bathing suit and a bright red bath towel.

Violet put on the bathing suit.

"But where did you get them?"

"I borrowed them," said the elephant, "from a clothesline I know. I promised to give them back later. And now that you're ready, let's go for a swim."

They raced each other into the water. Violet won because the elephant's big feet kept sinking into the wet sand.

They swam far out to sea. When Violet Katz got tired, the elephant lay on his back and she lay on his stomach.

"Do you get sunburnt?" she asked him.

"No," he said. "When I've had too much sun, I just go a very dark red."

He sucked up a trunkful of water and sprayed it into the air.

Then he bent his trunk the other way and Violet climbed onto his head and slid down into the water. Splash!

"I think it's time to get out," said the elephant. "I don't know about you but I'm getting hungry."

"Me too," agreed Violet.

They swam back to shore.

"There's a sandwich bar further down the beach and an ice-cream stand next door to it," said the elephant.

Violet put her hand in his trunk and they set off down the beach together.

They got to the sandwich bar and stood in the queue until it was their turn.

"I'm terribly hungry now," said Violet. "I'm going to have a cheese and tomato salad sandwich and an apple and some orange juice, and after that I'll have a big ice-cream."

"*I'm* going to have a hay and peanut butter sandwich and an apple and a bun and then a double size chocolate whopper ice-cream," said the elephant greedily. "Yum, yum. I'm starving."

Violet gave their orders to the man in the sandwich stall. He cut the bread and made the sandwiches. Then he wrapped everything up in paper bags.

"Here you are, Miss," he said. "That will be one pound and fifty-eight pence."

"It's one pound and fifty-eight pence," said Violet to the elephant. And she held out her hand for the money.

"I'm only an elephant," said the elephant. "I don't have any money. I thought you had some."

"I'm only a child. I don't have any money either. I thought *you* had some."

"I don't care which of you has the money as long as one of you pays me," said the man in the stall.

"We can't pay you. Neither of us has any money," said Violet.

"Well, I can't afford to give them away," said the man. "Tell you what, I'll put them on one side and you can go and get the money and come back for them later."

"Thank you," said Violet.

They went off together.

"I'm starving," said Violet. "I left in such a hurry I didn't have my breakfast."

"I'm hungry, too," moaned the elephant. "Elephants have to eat such a lot to keep fit and I haven't had any breakfast today either."

"Didn't your mother give you any?" said Violet.

"I don't have a mother," said the elephant sadly. "I ran away to join a circus when I was young and I quite lost contact with my family."

"Where do you live?" asked Violet.

"That's another thing," said the elephant. "I don't have a home of my own. I don't really belong anywhere. I was looking in your window this morning because it looked nice inside your house and your bedroom looked so comfortable."

"It is very nice," said Violet. "We don't have a car, though, because we can't afford it. And we don't have a television set either."

"What do you do in the evenings?"

"Sometimes we go for a walk, sometimes

my mother plays the harmonica to us or my father does acrobatic tricks, sometimes we have friends in to supper and sometimes we paint and colour in."

"It sounds wonderful," said the elephant wistfully. "Do you, by any chance, have a Christmas tree at Christmas?"

"Of course we do," said Violet. "*And* we have coloured lights and presents on it."

"How lovely," said the elephant.

"As a matter of fact, I'm getting hungrier every minute," Violet said, "and all this talk about home is making me even more ravenous. Shall we go home and get something?"

"I couldn't possibly take you home till I've had something to eat, I'm afraid."

"Well then," said Violet, "we'll just have to earn some money somehow."

"I could steal a bun with my trunk," said the elephant.

"You can't do that." Violet was definite. "That's not a good thing to do at all."

"But how will we make the money?"

"I'm considering," said Violet. "Ssh. Be quiet for a minute. I can't think if you're talking to me."

She sat down on the sand. Suddenly she jumped up.

"I've got it!" she cried. "You can give rides to children for ten pence. If you take three children each time, that will be thirty pence. And you'll only have to give six rides altogether."

"I don't want to," said the elephant. "I'm too tired. And, anyway, what are *you* going to do?"

"The publicity and the notices," said Violet.

"We haven't got any paper or chalk or anything to write on."

"We don't need it," Violet said triumphantly. "We've got the whole beach. Look!"

And she took a stick and wrote in the sand. ELEPHANT RIDES. 10p PER CHILD.

The elephant was doubtful.

"Supposing nobody comes."

"They will," said confident Violet.

"I'm exhausted," sighed the elephant.

"I know," said Violet. "And as soon as you've done one ride for three children, I'll run down to the ice-cream stall and bring you back a chocolate whopper."

"I'll do it," said the elephant.

"Roll up, roll up," called Violet. "Elephant rides! Elephant rides! Only ten pence per child. Roll up, roll up." She turned to the elephant. "Try to look more relaxed."

"I don't *feel* relaxed," muttered the elephant. "The thought of a lot of children clambering over me is very upsetting."

"Nonsense," said Violet briskly. "You'll love it. Besides, think what fun it will be for them."

A very old lady came up and peered at the notice in the sand.

"Elephant rides. How exciting," she said. "How much are they for adults?"

"We don't take *adults*," said Violet.

"Whyever not?" The old lady was surprised. "I'd love an elephant ride. Would he take me for twenty pence? I'm not very heavy."

"For twenty pence, he might," said Violet. "I'll ask him."

"I will, I will, as long as it gets me my chocolate whopper soon," groaned the elephant.

He swung the old lady up in his trunk. She

shrieked with excitement.

"Goodness me, it's exactly like the Big Wheel at the fair."

The elephant had just settled her on his back when a very fat man appeared.

"Can I have a ride, please?" he asked.

"You're not a child, I'm afraid," said Violet.

"Oh dear," said the fat man. "We adults are always being discriminated against. Can I have a ride if I pay thirty pence? That's fair."

"All right," said Violet, "you can."

The elephant sighed deeply, took a big breath and swung the fat man up onto his back.

The fat man giggled.

"There's a wonderful view from up here," he said.

"Splendid, isn't it?" said the old lady.

"Marvellous!" said the fat man. "I haven't had an elephant ride since I was a boy."

Violet patted the elephant's trunk.

"We've got fifty pence already," she whispered. "You *are* doing well."

A man and a woman came up together. They looked exactly alike except that the man wore a striped shirt and trousers and the woman wore a striped blouse and skirt. They both wore identical straw hats and black shoes.

"Can you take us?" they said together.

"One," said Violet, "but not both. One of you will have to wait."

"But we must both go," they said in chorus. "We're twins. We do everything together all the time."

"Dear, dear," trumpeted the elephant. "I suppose I shall have to take them, but it's very bad for my back. And I'm quite worn out already."

Violet took a deep breath.

"He'll take you," she said, "but it will be fifty pence each."

"Done!" said the twins.

The elephant curled his trunk round them and lifted them up in the air.

"What fun," they cried. "This *is* exciting."

"I'm ready to go," announced the elephant.

"Just a minute," said Violet, "there's something shining in the sand."

She reached down and picked it up. It was a ten pence piece.

"We've got one pound and sixty pence," she said proudly to the elephant. "I'll go and pay for the food and bring it back while you take them for their ride."

"Don't forget the ice-cream," the elephant reminded and he lumbered off with everyone calling out eagerly on his back.

Violet set off for the sandwich stall.

"Here you are again," said the sandwich

man. "Got your money now, have you?"

"Yes," said Violet. "Here it is. Thank you for keeping our sandwiches."

"Pleasure," said the man as he handed her the package.

Violet Katz set off along the beach humming to herself. She had got halfway back when, suddenly, she had a terrible thought. She had spent all the money except two pence and she hadn't got any ice-cream.

"Oh dear!" she cried, aghast. "I promised the elephant and I completely forgot and now I haven't got any money left."

And she sat down in the sun to think.

A boy came by with a double vanilla ice-cream cone.

"How much did that cost?" asked Violet.

"Twenty-five pence," said the boy.

"Fifty pence for two," thought Violet, and aloud she said,

"Would you like to see me stand on my head?"

"Oh yes," said the boy.

"It will cost you five pence," said Violet.

"I think my brother would like to see you

too," said the boy. "I'll just go and get him."

Violet wrote a large notice in the sand.

PERFORMING GIRL. HEADSTANDS, ACROBATICS, DANCING AND WHISTLING. 5p PER PERSON.

A crowd began to collect.

"When does it start?" someone asked.

"As soon as we have ten or twelve people," said Violet.

"There are fourteen people here already," said a man.

Violet collected the money. Seventy pence.

Another man came up and paid his five pence. Seventy-five pence.

They made a circle round Violet and she began. She danced, she whistled, she tumbled and forward rolled and finally she stood on her head.

All the people clapped and cheered. Violet bowed.

"Thank you very much," she said and bowed again. Then she picked up her seventy-five pence and made her way quickly to the ice-cream stall.

"Two double whoppers with chocolate

sticks, please," she said to the man.

"Coming up," said the man.

Violet took the ice-creams and ran as fast as she could along the beach.

The elephant was sitting in the sand looking very sulky.

"I thought you were never coming back," he said crossly.

"Here," said Violet. "I've brought you a double chocolate whopper with a chocolate flake stick."

The elephant shot out his trunk and seized the ice-cream.

"*Delicious!!!*" he breathed. "I needed that. Thank you."

He smiled at Violet.

"Let's have another swim."

"After my lunch," said Violet. "I've got to eat."

"Swim first," said the elephant, "then eat."

So they splashed into the water and cooled off.

When they came out they ate their lunch.

"Oh," sighed Violet, "I feel *much* better."

The elephant yawned contentedly.

"There's *nothing* like a hay and peanut butter sandwich," he murmured.

They lay under a tree and went to sleep.

When they woke it was still sunny. First they built a sandcastle and made a moat around it, then the elephant sucked up water in his trunk to fill it.

Suddenly, there was a shout from further down the beach and the old lady who had had the elephant ride came rushing up.

"Thank goodness!" she called. "I've been looking for you everywhere. I enjoyed that ride so much I went home and emptied my money box and got out my tutu and I've come back for some more. I used to be in the circus when I was a girl and I want to see if I can still ride an elephant bare-back, standing on one leg. Will you let me try?"

"Of course," said Violet and the elephant together.

The old lady tipped a pile of money onto the sand, gave Violet her bag to hold and went off to change. She came back in a beautiful pink and white tutu.

"It's very old," she said proudly, "but it still fits."

She lifted her arms high into the air and the elephant wrapped his trunk round her waist and raised her up and onto his back. The old lady took a minute to get her balance, then, slowly, she stood on her left toe and lifted her right leg high in the air behind her.

"Wonderful!" cried Violet.

The elephant moved carefully forward: the old lady went on balancing beautifully on his back.

All along the beach they went. People came running out of the water and dropped whatever they were doing to come and watch.

"Magnificent! Amazing! Fantastic!" they cheered.

The old lady was overjoyed.

"I haven't had such a wonderful time for years," she said. "Come home to tea with me."

So Violet and the elephant went to tea at the old lady's enormous and beautiful house. They sat on the lawn because the elephant couldn't get in through the front door.

When they had finished, Violet said, "I really think I must be getting home. Ma and Pa will be wondering where I am, and they'll be worried if I don't get back soon."

The elephant got up.

"Thank you for a delicious tea," he trumpeted.

The old lady waved goodbye and made them promise to visit if ever they were at the seaside again.

"And now," said the elephant, "home! But first I have to return those clothes, so you'd better get back into your nightie."

"I'll feel very silly in my nightie at five o'clock," objected Violet.

"Well, you can't wear nothing at all," said the elephant. Then he had an idea.

"We've got lots of money from the old lady. We could go and buy you some new clothes and I could have a striped scarf. I've always wanted a striped scarf."

Violet was delighted.

"What a wonderful idea."

So off they went.

The man in the shop was rather surprised to see Violet in her nightie but he sold her a set of clothes and a striped scarf.

Violet put on her new trousers and T-shirt and asked him to wrap up her nightgown, then she walked up the elephant's trunk and sat down on his back and they raced off home.

The elephant was very quiet on the way.

"What's the matter?" said Violet.

"Nothing," said the elephant. Then he said miserably, "Well, I may as well tell you. I wish *I* had a home to go back to."

"Where do you sleep at night?" asked Violet.

"Usually in a field, if it's warm, and in a

barn or some sort of old building, if it's wet. But I'm always moving round. I'd like a *proper* home of my own," sighed the elephant.

"I think you'd better come home with me," said Violet.

"But what about your parents?" The elephant was anxious. "Maybe they won't want an elephant."

"Of course they'll want an elephant," Violet declared. "Why shouldn't they? Come on, let's go faster."

The elephant was going at a great pace. Soon they saw Violet's house ahead of them with Mr Katz looking out of the window.

"Ma, Ma," yelled Mr Katz, "come quickly. Violet has just ridden home on the back of a big *red* elephant."

Mrs Katz dropped her spoon in the home-brew mix.

"I don't believe it. You're seeing things, Pa."

"I am not. Just you look outside the front door."

At that moment the elephant poked his long red trunk through the window. Mrs Katz screamed.

"Have you got a bun, Ma?" called Violet from the elephant's back.

Mrs Katz took a wholemeal loaf from the cupboard and gave it to the elephant.

Violet slid down the elephant's trunk, through the window and landed on the kitchen floor.

"Violet Katz," said her mother wearily, "this morning you rode off without telling us on the back of a large pink elephant and now you've come home on big *red* one. What HAVE you been doing?"

"As a matter of fact," said Violet, "I've been to the seaside for the day. And the elephant *was* pink but he went red in the sun."

"The seaside!" cried her parents together. "It's *miles* away."

"I know. But elephants move quickly."

"And you went in your nightie," said Mrs Katz.

"It's all your fault for not listening to me when I told you about the elephant. No one believed me," said Violet. "And I went in my nightie because I didn't have time to change. But just wait a minute."

She climbed up the elephant's trunk, out through the window and onto his back, then slid down again carrying a bundle in her arms.

"Look!"

"What is it?" cried the Katzes.

"My nightie," said Violet. "The elephant and I worked on the beach and earned the money for the new clothes I'm wearing. *And* here's a new bathing towel. And I've had lunch and been swimming and I've had a *lovely* day. Now where can we keep my

155

elephant?"

"*Keep it?*" shrieked Mr Katz. "We can't keep an ELEPHANT."

"Why not?" asked Violet calmly.

"Because we can't, that's why."

"Well, it's him or me," said Violet. "Either he comes here or I go off with him."

"We couldn't bear to lose you," sighed her mother. "It was bad enough worrying about you all day today, so I suppose we'll have to keep the elephant. But where on earth can we put him?"

"We can't keep him," said Mr Katz, "we're not allowed to have pets in this house."

"He's not a *pet*," said Violet scornfully. "How could anyone call him a pet? He's a vehicle. I've been riding on him all day."

"I suppose he *is* a vehicle," said Mr Katz doubtfully.

"Of course he is." Violet was positive. "And if he had number plates, he'd definitely be a vehicle."

"I do have a pair of number plates in the cupboard, actually," said Mrs Katz. "They're left over from my motorcycle. When I sold it, the woman who bought it wanted new ones with her initials on so I kept the old ones."

She got them out.

"But how will we hang them on the elephant?" wondered Mr Katz.

"Easy," said Violet. "We put a string through the holes at each end and hang one over his tail and one over his trunk."

"Do you think we could go shopping on him?" asked Mrs Katz.

"Yes, of course. And we could go to the seaside quite often," said Violet. "Now, where's he going to sleep?"

"That's a problem," said Mr Katz. He thought hard.

"There's a basement under the house," said Mrs Katz. "I used to keep my motorbike in there."

"The door's too small," said Violet. "We couldn't get an elephant through a little door like that."

"What a pity," said Mr Katz. "Because the basement would be perfect."

The pink elephant put his red trunk lovingly round Violet's shoulder. She climbed out to scratch his ears.

"Can I stay?" he asked.

"We're just sorting out where you can sleep," explained Violet.

"I'm not fussy," said the elephant humbly. "Any old stable will do me."

"We don't actually have a stable," said Violet. "That's the problem. But don't worry. We'll solve it."

She clambered back inside.

They sat round the table, still thinking. Suddenly Mrs Katz thumped the table hard and jumped to her feet.

"I have it! The perfect answer."

"What? What?" cried Violet and her father.

"Just wait a minute," said Mrs Katz mysteriously.

She went out of the room and was back two minutes later with her tool kit.

"If we can't get Violet's elephant in through the basement door, we'll have to get him in through the basement roof."

"But the basement is under the house. The basement roof is just below the kitchen floor." Mr Katz was puzzled.

"Exactly," said Mrs Katz. "I am now going to make the kitchen floor into a trapdoor and we can put a ramp down into the basement for Violet's elephant."

"It's a wonderful idea," said Mr Katz slowly, "but how do we get the elephant through the front door of the house?"

"Easy," said Mrs Katz. "Simple. We take out the bay windows and put them back in afterwards. And tomorrow I'll knock out the small basement door and build a big sliding up-and-over door so the elephant can get in and out easily. But at least tonight he won't have to sleep outdoors in the cold."

Violet took a hammer, Mrs Katz took a crowbar, Mr Katz took a saw, the elephant took some nails, and they started work.

In no time at all they had turned the kitchen floor into a trap door.

In a very short time they had made a ramp. And finally they took out the windows.

And then, with a lot of pushing and pulling and to-ing and fro-ing, they finally got the elephant through the gap inside the house. Mr Katz lifted the trap door, and the elephant walked down the ramp and into his basement.

"How delightful," he smiled. "A place of my own at last."

Mr and Mrs Katz and Violet put the windows back in place and put the tools away.

"And now," said Mr Katz, "supper."

"Oh good," said the elephant. "What are we eating?"

Mr and Mrs Katz and Violet looked at one another.

"Oh dear," said Violet. "I forgot about his food."

"What does he eat?" asked Mrs Katz.

Violet looked worried. "Hay and stale buns and occasionally peanuts."

They sat down to think hard again.

Suddenly Mr Katz jumped up and banged on the table.

"I've got it! I've got it," he shouted.

"What? What?" cried Mrs Katz and Violet.

"Simple," said Mr Katz happily. "Every Thursday, the elephant can do free deliveries for the bakery, and in return they can give him all their stale buns every night. And the hay's no problem at all. Hay is just dried grass.

Violet and her elephant can collect the grass cuttings once a week from the park."

"How clever," said Mrs Katz.

"But what do we feed him tonight?" asked Violet.

"Scones and crumpets, of course," said Mrs Katz. "Your father was just going to bake some when you came in."

"So I was," said Mr Katz. "How forgetful of me."

And he leaned down into the basement and called to the elephant.

"With or without cheese?"

"What?" said the elephant.

"Your scones," said Mr Katz.

"Oh, with, please," said the elephant.

Mr Katz put on his apron. Mrs Katz swept up the woodshavings.

They looked at Violet.

"Ma," said Mr Katz, "I think we're very lucky to have an interesting daughter like Violet."

"Pa," said Mrs Katz, "I think I agree with you."

Violet smiled at them both.

And down in the basement Violet's pink
elephant trumpeted happily in his new home.

THE ENCHANTED TOAD

There was once a king who had a daughter called Princess Grizelda. Princess Grizelda was rather quiet and didn't say very much but she was very very stubborn and determined once she had decided on something.

The Queen, her mother, had left their home at the palace many years before, when Grizelda was a small girl, to seek her fortune as a racing driver, so the king had had to bring up his daughter by himself.

"Grizelda," he said to her one day, "I have a serious problem to discuss with you. Come into the blue drawing room."

The Princess put down her bow and arrows and followed him.

"What is it, Papa?"

"Grizelda," said the king, "it's time you were married."

"But I'm only fourteen, Papa," protested the princess.

"What do you mean – 'only fourteen'?" said the king. "Fourteen's quite old enough to be married."

"But I don't *want* to be married, Papa."

"Well, sooner or later you'll have to be," said the king, "so why not now?"

"I don't know if I ever want to be married, Papa."

"What nonsense!" cried the king. "Everyone wants to be married. Why I was married at twenty and your mother was married at fifteen."

"I know," said the princess, "and when she was eighteen she went off to race cars and we haven't seen her since."

"Well, she always sends you a birthday present," said the king defensively.

"Yes, I know, but I'd rather *see* her sometimes."

"Grizelda," said the king, "you are not to talk about Mama. You know it only upsets me. I'm not going to listen if you do. And I want you, in fact, I'm ordering you, to start thinking about who you want to marry. Because if you don't come up with some good suggestions yourself, I shall have to choose for you."

And he stormed out of the blue drawing room.

Grizelda thought about all the neighbouring princes. She really couldn't face the thought of marrying any of them.

"Well," she said to herself, "I shall just have to do something about Papa."

"So," said the king at dinner, "have you decided, Grizelda?"

"Really, Papa, you only asked me to think about it five hours ago."

The king stamped his foot and his soup plate rattled.

"Five hours is long enough for anyone."

"Not for me," said the princess calmly.

"And you've spilt your soup."

"Oh, be quiet!" shouted the king and he slammed out of the royal dining room.

The princess ate the rest of her dinner in thoughtful silence.

Next day she had breakfast in her room, got dressed in her best golden dress and slipped outdoors in her blue silk cloak.

"Your Highness," said the page as she passed him on the stairs, "His Majesty has asked several kings and queens from neighbouring kingdoms to lunch with him today and he particularly wants you to be present."

"Thank you," said the princess. "I'll be there." And to herself she thought, "He's asked them so he can marry me off to one of their sons."

And she carried on downstairs even faster.

She stayed in the gardens for an hour or two, then slipped back into the palace and up to her bedroom unnoticed. She had just enough time to sort out a few things before lunch.

There was a blast of trumpets from downstairs.

"That'll be the heralds announcing the arrival of the other monarchs," sighed Princess Grizelda and she smoothed her golden dress, picked up something from her bed and set off for the royal reception room.

"The Princess Grizelda," announced a herald.

"My dear," said the king and he walked up and embraced her warmly. "Behave yourself, please," he muttered in her ear.

"I always do, Papa," said the princess.

The king led her forward. "This," he said, "is my daughter, Grizelda, my only child. In due course she will inherit the kingdom and I feel she is now of an age to be married."

The royal guests smiled at her. The princess smiled back. She took a deep breath.

"Papa," she said loudly, taking a step forward, "I've found a husband for myself."

"Really, Grizelda?" said the king. "You surprise me. And who is the lucky young man?"

"I met him in the garden this morning," said the princess. "He's waiting outside in the hall."

"Let him come in!" commanded the king.

"Now we can all see this mysterious fellow. 'Met him in the garden,' indeed! Young girls are so fanciful."

The princess went out to the hall, picked up a small box she had deposited there and carried it in.

"Well?" demanded the king. "Where is he then?"

The princess lifted the lid of the box.

"Here, Papa."

The king looked in the box.

"That's a toad!"

"Yes, I know, Papa. I've fallen in love with it and I'm going to marry it."

"GRIZELDA," thundered the king.

"Lunch is served, Sire," announced the footman appearing at the door.

One of the visiting kings leaned over to Grizelda's father and whispered in his ear, "I shouldn't discourage her if I were you. It will almost certainly be a prince under enchantment."

The king was doubtful.

"Are you sure?"

"They always are," said the visiting king.

"Let her have him on the table at lunch and have your Court Enchanter change him back later on."

"What a splendid idea," said the king. "Thank you. I hadn't thought of that."

"There have been dozens of cases exactly like it," said the visiting king.

So the Princess Grizelda took her toad in to lunch and it sat by her golden plate as she fed it with tiny scraps of her own food.

The visitors left in the early afternoon. Grizelda shook hands with them all and smiled prettily. The toad looked at them with its unblinking eyes.

The king felt a light touch on his shoulder.

"Don't forget. Get the enchanter in right away," murmured his friend.

Grizelda's father nodded.

"Many thanks," he said gratefully.

"Don't mention it," said the visiting king.

The princess took her toad into the library. She was examining its warts when a herald arrived with a message that she and the toad were wanted in the throne room.

"The throne room!" The princess was impressed. "Something special must be happening."

"His Majesty is in full regalia," said the

herald importantly.

"Really? It must be something vital then. I wonder what it can be?" said the princess and, picking up her toad, she set off along the palace corridor.

The throne room door was opened by a page but inside were the King, the Lord Chamberlain, the Court Jester, the Chief Judge and the Court Enchanter. The Court Enchanter was considered one of the best wizards in the world. He was always going off to perform difficult spells or to change people back into their normal shapes or to magick someone or something somewhere. People said he could conjure up all sorts of wonderful things and nobody wanted to get on the wrong side of him because it was reputed that he had once put a bad spell on someone who had offended him and caused lizards to jump out of her mouth every time she opened it.

Grizelda went into the room.

"Good afternoon, Papa," she said and nodded at his retinue.

"Good afternoon, my dear," said the king. He looked at the toad, swallowed, and said with a great effort, "And how is my future son-in-law this afternoon?"

"Very well, thank you, Papa."

"Good," said the king.

"Would you like to stroke him, Papa?"

"No thanks!" said the king hastily. "Ah, I'm sure he's, ah, very, ah, friendly, yes, I'm sure he's got a wonderful nature and so on, but, ah, I don't think I'll stroke him just yet, thank you, Grizelda.

"Now," he went on, "the reason I've brought you down here is because I happen to believe your toad, that is, my son-in-law to be, is really a prince under enchantment."

The princess was very disappointed.

"Oh no, Papa, I hope not!"

"Look here," said the king. "Don't be ridiculous, Grizelda. I mean you can get toads anywhere but princes are another thing altogether. I'll get you another toad as a wedding present if you want. And that's a promise. Now bring that toad over here and put him on the small table."

Grizelda put down her toad in front of the enchanter.

The enchanter looked at her with piercing green eyes.

"Stand back, Your Highness," he ordered. Taking a huge red silk handkerchief from one pocket of his robe, and a wand from the other, he dropped the handkerchief over the toad, threw a powder from another pocket into a glass of water, poured the water over the handkerchief, then waved his wand over it, muttering strangely to himself all the time.

There was sudden flash of pink smoke and a dull boom, the handkerchief and the toad disappeared, and in their place stood a white rabbit.

The princess was overjoyed.

"A rabbit! Oh, Papa, how wonderful! I've always wanted a rabbit."

"Not for a *husband*!" bellowed the king, enraged.

And to the enchanter he said nastily, "You'll have to do something considerably better than that!"

The enchanter turned his piercing green eyes towards the king.

"Patience, Your Highness. These things are very skilled and take time."

"I can see that," said the king bitterly.

The enchanter pulled out another handkerchief, a blue one this time, and laid it over the rabbit.

"Oh no, please don't." The princess was distressed.

The enchanter felt deep in his robe, pulled out a tiny top hat, and presented it to her.

"Here you are," he said. "Put your hand in there."

Grizelda could only get two fingers into the hat because it was so small. Feeling something soft and furry, she pulled at it.

Out popped the tiniest rabbit she had ever seen.

"For you," said the enchanter. "A present to make up for losing this one."

"Thank you," said the princess and she tucked the baby rabbit back in the hat for safe keeping and put the hat in her pocket.

The enchanter was busy with his spell. He had taken out a large book from behind the throne, a book Grizelda was sure had never been there before, and was studying it intently.

Suddenly he leaned towards the king.

"Excuse me, Your Majesty," he said and reaching behind the king's ear, pulled out a large lemon.

"Oh dear," he said and, from behind the king's other ear, pulled out an enormous black spider.

"Stop it *at once*!" commanded the king. "And that's an order."

"Sorry, Your Majesty," said the enchanter. "I just thought you'd like to know they were there."

"Thank you for that consideration," said the king. "Now get on with the job."

The enchanter plucked a star from out of the air above his head, laid it on the blue handkerchief, twirled three times round on his toes and shouted "Abracadabra!"

There was a blinding flash of green light and, lo and behold, a beautiful red sports car appeared before them.

"My gosh!" breathed Grizelda.

The Lord Chancellor sighed enviously. "I'd like that."

The king looked very hard at the enchanter. "I see: a sports car."

"Well, yes," said the enchanter. "I told Your Majesty these things take time."

"Look," said the king through clenched teeth, "I cannot have a sports car as a son-in-law. The princess cannot marry a *sports car*."

His voice rose to a shriek. "*Whoever heard of a kingdom ruled by a sports car?*"

"A passing bagatelle, Your Majesty," said the enchanter. "We're almost there now."

"It is a very beautiful sports car," said the princess.

"Grizelda…" said the king warningly.

The Lord Chamberlain broke in. "Your Majesty, the enchanter is about to try again."

"He'd better," said the king.

The enchanter took out a checked table-cloth from the back pocket of his robe and flung it over the sports car.

The Lord Chamberlain sighed. "What a pity."

The king shot him a furious look.

The enchanter lifted three lizards out of a banqueting dish on the regalia table and laid them on the cloth. He took a vial of red liquid from his sleeve, shook it over the lizards and waved his wand low over them.

A tongue of flame shot into the air. Everybody screamed and jumped back.

The smoke cleared and there before them lay – a fish finger.

"NO, NO, NO, NO," screeched the king. "THERE IS NO SUCH THING AS A KINGDOM RULED BY A FISH FINGER! I'm *not* having a fish finger as a son-in-law. I'd rather have a toad." He pointed at the enchanter. "Take him away!" he shouted. "Off with his head and bring it to me on a plate! It'll be a pleasure, I can tell you."

"Papa!" The princess was shocked. "What a *terrible* thing to say."

The enchanter burst into tears. He reached into his other sleeve and brought out a placard saying,

"WIFE AND SIX CHILDREN TO SUPPORT."

"You won't get my sympathy *that* way," said the king. "My mind is made up. Take him away!"

Princess Grizelda jumped to her feet and stood in front of her father.

"I won't have it, Papa," she cried. "This was all your idea in the first place and it wasn't even your toad. It was mine. Of course you're not going to chop off the enchanter's head. You're going to give him one last chance to succeed and if he doesn't, you're going to send him on a month's holiday."

"That's just encouraging him to fail," said the king.

"Honestly, Sire," said the enchanter, "it was a temporary setback. I've prepared my next and final spell now. I *am* in the entertainment business, Sire, after all."

"Entertainment!" exploded the king. "You call this entertainment?"

"Stop it, at once, both of you," ordered the princess. And turning to the enchanter she said, "Please try again."

"And get it right this time," snorted the king.

"I will," said the enchanter.

He pulled a purple silken cloth with golden stars on it from the Lord Chamberlain's trouser leg and laid it over the fish finger. Then he reached inside his own mouth, pulled out a tonsil and placed that on the cloth.

"Yuk!" said the king. "How disgusting!"

"But effective, Sire," said the enchanter. "And now, please, absolute silence."

He bent down on his knees, crossed his

fingers, his toes and his eyes and breathed on the tonsil.

The tonsil quivered and grew and grew. The purple cloth with golden stars rose and flapped and shook until it seemed to fill the room. There was a boom of thunder and a light like the sun dazzled them all.

"How beautiful," murmured the princess.

Suddenly there was a jolt and a bang and without warning they all flew up to the ceiling and fell to the floor again. The room grew dark.

"Sorry about this," came the enchanter's voice through the gloom. "Nearly there."

A misty cloud was gathering in the middle of the room. A dim human shape was forming inside it.

The enchanter sighed inaudibly with relief. The king muttered, "At last."

And the Princess Grizelda said to herself, "I do hope this prince is nice and he likes having fun."

The cloud began to dispel, the light slowly returned to normal and the figure emerged more clearly until it stood visible to them all.

"GOOD HEAVENS!" bellowed the king. "It's Marguerite!"

"Hello, darling," said the figure.

"Mother!" shouted Grizelda and threw herself into the stranger's arms.

"And where have *you* been for the last eleven years then?" said the king.

"Oh, Arthur," said the queen, holding Grizelda tightly, "don't go on and on, please. I thought you'd be so glad to see me again. I've been away seeking my fortune, of course. I'm an extremely famous racing driver."

"Well, *I've* never heard of you," said the king, "and I've checked the racing lists every time there's been a Grand Prix."

"Oh, Arthur. Have you?" The queen was touched. "That is romantic of you."

The king blushed.

"But," explained the queen, "I had to race under an assumed name otherwise people might have thought my winning was favouritism." She hugged Grizelda. "It's so wonderful to see you at last, my darling. I've wanted and wanted to come home, but I knew I couldn't until I'd proved myself. And I've finally done it."

The Princess Grizelda clung tighter to her mother's neck.

"Oh, Mama, I'm so glad you're back at last."

"What I don't understand," said the king, "is if you've reached the peak of your career, what on earth you were doing in the palace disguised as a toad. And then to put me through that dreadful business of the rabbit and the sports car and the fish finger. It's a wonder I'm not grey with worry and strain."

"I couldn't help it," said the queen. She turned to the enchanter. "It was such a strong spell. You did marvellously well to break it at all."

The enchanter looked modest.

"It was nothing, Your Highness."

"It was everything to *me*," said the queen. "I could have just about coped with spending the rest of my life as a pet rabbit or a sports car and at least I would have been at the palace. But a fish finger! I ask you? Here one day and gobbled up the next. I was so terrified, I was shaking in my breadcrumbs."

"Oh, Mama," breathed Grizelda, "just imagine if the enchanter had failed and we'd eaten you up for tea."

Her eyes filled with tears at the thought.

"Well, we didn't," said the king, "so stop crying, Grizelda."

He put his arm round the queen and kissed her cheek.

"I'm glad you've come back."

"I shall never go off again now," said the queen, "though I had some fun while I was racing."

"Will you tell me all about it?" asked Grizelda eagerly.

"Later," promised the queen.

"We must have a banquet and a party to celebrate your return," said the king. "But there's still one thing I don't understand. Why were you a toad?"

"Well," said the queen, "I was racing very well and it was obvious I was going to win the title. The only person anywhere near as good was a driver who'd been a wizard and had given it up for racing. And when I had won and it came to the presentation of the prizes, he was so jealous that he cast a spell over me and changed me into a toad, and it took me seven months to hop back here to the palace.

But it wasn't till Grizelda found me that anyone noticed me at all, and, of course, you know the rest of the story."

"Amazing," said the king.

"That wizard should be punished," said the Chief Judge.

"He will be," said the king. "I'll make a point of it."

"Well, if everyone is happy now," said the enchanter, "I'd quite like to be getting off home to my own family…"

"Just a moment," said the king sternly. "You promised me a husband for the princess and I haven't got one. She can't marry her mother."

"With respect, Sire," said the enchanter, "*you* asked me if I could change a toad into a prince and I said I'd do my best. I rather thought," he went on huffily, "that I'd done better than my best, but of course if Your Majesty disagrees…"

"You've done *marvellously*," cried the queen, "and I shall personally see about a reward."

The enchanter smiled.

"I still don't know how I'm going to get

Grizelda a husband though," muttered the king.

"A husband!" The queen was incredulous. "What does she want a *husband* for? She's only fourteen."

"I don't want a husband," put in Grizelda hastily.

"I should think *not*," said the queen. "I've never heard such nonsense. I married young, and look what happened to me. You're surely not encouraging her, Arthur?"

"Well, what else is she going to do?" said the king.

"What do you want to do, Grizelda?" asked her mother.

Grizelda thought for a bit.

"What I'd like, Mama," she said finally, "is to stay here with you for a while and play with my rabbit, and the toad Papa has promised me, and then there's something else I really want to do."

"And what is that?"

"I hope you won't think it's silly," said the princess, "but I'd simply *love* to be an astronaut. I've always wanted to be one."

"I've never heard of anything so ridiculous," said the king.

"I think it's a wonderfully exciting idea," said the queen, "and you should certainly be allowed to try it. And now, Arthur," she continued, turning to the king, "if it's possible, and I'm sure it should be, I'd love something to eat. I'm thoroughly sick of slugs and snails and worms."

"Oh, my dear," cried the king remorsefully, "of course, of course. I'm so sorry. I completely forgot about it in the shock of the moment. Yes. At once. Let's all three of us have a special celebration meal together tonight. I'm so delighted to have you home again."

"And so am I, Mama," murmured the Princess Grizelda, snuggling up to her mother.

"It seems to me," said the enchanter to himself, "that this time I've made an entirely satisfactory job of things."

And, wrapping his cloak tightly round himself, he waved a hasty goodbye to everyone and slipped out of the palace off home to his own supper.

HIPPO GHOST

The House at the End of Ferry Road

The house at the end of Ferry Road has just been built. So it can't be haunted, can it...?
Martin Oliver

Beware! This House is Haunted

Jessica is sure one of her stepbrothers wrote the note. But soon there are more notes ... strange midnight laughter ... floating objects... Perhaps the house really is haunted...

This House is Haunted Too!

It's starting all over again. First the note, and now strange things are happening to Jessica's family... The mischievous ghost is back – and worse than ever. Will they never be rid of it...?
Lance Salway

The Children Next Door

Laura longs to make friends with the children next door. When she finally plucks up courage, she meets Zilla – but she's an only child. So who are the other children she's seen playing in next door's garden...?
Jean Ure

And coming soon...

Ghostly Music
Richard Brown

Summer Visitors
Carol Barton

HiPPO ANiMAL

*If you like animals, then you'll love
Hippo Animal Stories!*

Thunderfoot
Deborah van der Beek
When Mel finds the enormous, neglected horse
Thunderfoot, she doesn't know it will change her
life for ever...

Vanilla Fudge
Deborah van der Beek
When Lizzie and Hannah fall in love with the same
dog, neither of them will give up without a fight...

A Foxcub Named Freedom
Brenda Jobling
An injured vixen nudges her young son away from her.
She can sense danger and cares nothing for herself –
only for her son's freedom...

Pirate the Seal
Brenda Jobling
Ryan's always been lonely – but then he meets Pirate and at last he has a real friend...

Animal Rescue
Bette Paul
Can Tessa help save the badgers of Delves Wood from destruction?

Take Six Puppies
Bette Paul
Anna knows she shouldn't get attached to the six new puppies at the Millington Farm Dog Sanctuary, but surely it can't hurt to get just a *little* bit fond of them...

HIPPO FANTASY

Lose yourself in a whole new world, a world where anything is possible – from wizards and dragons, to time travel and new civilizations... Gripping, thrilling, scary and funny by turns, these Hippo Fantasy titles will hold you captivated to the very last page.

The Night of Wishes
Michael Ende

Malcolm and the Cloud-Stealer
Douglas Hill

The Crystal Keeper
James Jauncey

The Wednesday Wizard
Sherryl Jordan

Ratspell
Paddy Mounter

Rowan of Rin
Rowan and the Travellers
Emily Rodda

The Practical Princess
Jay Williams